PULP
Literature

PULP
Literature

PULP LITERATURE PRESS
Issue No. 17, Winter 2018

PULP *Literature*

Pulp Literature Press, Publisher
Jennifer Landels, Managing Editor
Mel Anastasiou, Acquisitions Editor
Susan Pieters, Developmental Editor
Janet Eastwood, Assistant Editor,
Daniel Cowper, Poetry Editor
Amanda Bidnall, Copy Editor
Mary Rykov, Proofreader
Kris Sayer, Graphic Designer
Adam Fout, Marketing Director
Winston Le, Publicity Intern
Jessica Fabrizius, Editorial Intern
For advertising rates direct inquiries to info@pulpliterature.com.

Cover painting, *Patron Saint of the Inevitable Death of the Universe*, by Britt-Lise Newstead. Illustrations for 'Afloat' by Gabriel Craven & Mikayla Fawcett. Illustrations for *Allaigna's Song: Aria* by JM Landels. All other illustrations by Mel Anastasiou.

Pulp Literature: ISSN 2292-2164 (Print), ISSN 2292-2172 (Online), Issue No. 17, Winter 2018.

Published quarterly by Pulp Literature Press, 8540 Elsmore Road, Richmond, BC, Canada V7C 2A1, pulpliterature.com at $15.00 per copy. Annual subscription $50.00 in Canada, $66.00 in continental USA, $82.00 elsewhere. Printed in Victoria, BC, Canada, by First Choice Books / Victoria Bindery. Copyright © 2018 Pulp Literature Press.

Pulp Literature Press gratefully acknowledges the support of the Canada Council for the Arts.

Canada Council   Conseil des arts
for the Arts   du Canada

Pulp Literature is a proud member of the Magazine Association of BC.

TABLE OF CONTENTS

FROM THE PULP LIT PULPIT

Winter Storytelling

At this time of year, when the days are at their shortest, the darkness seems personal. Luckily we all have a stack of books leaning up against a favourite armchair or tucked to hand beneath the bed to carry our thoughts out of the gloom and remind us of the seeds of hope that lie dormant, waiting to sprout when the cold relents.

We tuck feet under a throw and adjust the lamp's beam. We follow our literary moods — fantasy, mystery, speculative fiction in twelve-volume series, or short stories. Short fiction is structurally ideal for long winter nights, offering a complete arc in the time it takes to sip a warm cup of something and giving us a tale to relish and retell at candlelit suppers when work fills the daylight hours and politics pall.

It's been our pleasure to assemble for your reading enjoyment this slate of brilliant reads.

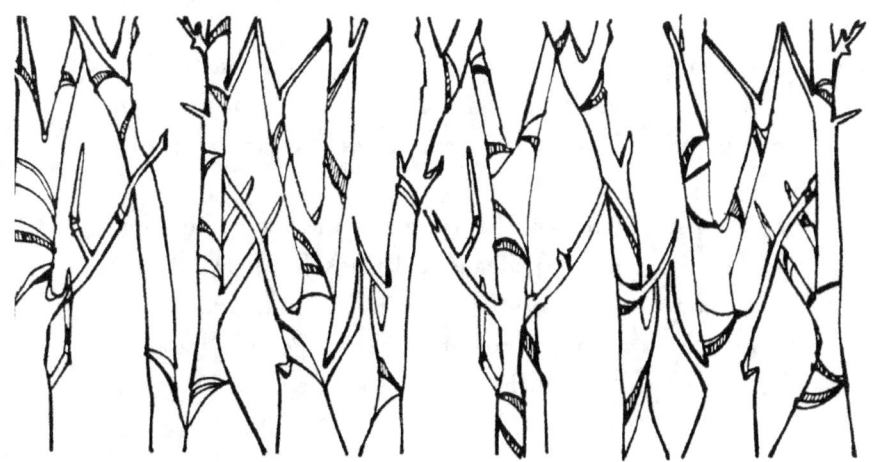

*I*N THIS ISSUE

Featured author **JJ Lee**'s 'Desdemone' opens our winter issue with an exquisite Edwardian haunting of a most personal kind.

Emily Osborne's poem 'Devonian' sends us across time, deep into the primeval world; needles inform lives in **John Davies**'s 'Tattoo'; **Kelli Allen**'s 'You don't know your life anyway' gives us a complicated relationship in a few great lines; and 'Sea Changes', by **Matilda Berke**, weaves Celtic myths with water.

With 'One Safe Place', **Erin Slaughter** takes us on a road trip we'll never forget, and 'We Come Back Different' from **AJ Odasso** gives us the first half of a gripping steampunk tale of strange science and mysterious disappearances in an alternate past.

'Embers' by **Misha Handman** tells of an old woman's last struggle against the darkness she's been fighting for a lifetime, and **Anat Rabkin**'s 'For the Love of Grey' reaffirms that attitude is everything, even in Hell.

In two tales that demonstrate the power of words, **Susan Pieter**'s 'Lineman' puts readers up a ladder among live wires, and **Soramimi Hanarejima**'s 'Theft of Confidence' takes language to a new level.

In this issue we present the winning stories of the Hummingbird Flash Fiction Prize. **Jeanette Topar**'s 'Just Down the Hall' opens a door to something unexpected. And our first-prize story, **William Kaufmann**'s 'The Bruised Peach', pleases as it alters perception through a strange encounter.

Spencer Stevens takes another stab at happiness with the help of the Seven Swans pub in the fifth instalment of **Mel Anastasiou**'s *Hertfordshire Pub Mysteries*, 'The Bridgewater Canal Mystery'. And our heroine is up to her sword hilt in new dangers in the latest episode of *Allaigna's Song: Aria* by **JM Landels**.

It's the end of the world, but skies are blue in the cheerful post-apocalyptic comic 'Afloat' by **Gabriel Craven** and **Mikayla Fawcett**.

We hope you'll find the same delight and satisfaction in reading this brilliant selections that we did in finding them.

All our best wishes,
Jen, Mel, & Sue

DESDEMONE

JJ Lee

JJ Lee *presents a Christmas ghost story every year on CBC Radio in British Columbia. He mentors a non-fiction workshop at Simon Fraser University's The Writer's Studio. His memoir,* The Measure of a Man: The Story of a Father, a Son, and a Suit, *was a finalist for a Governor-General's Award for Literature. This is his third short story for* Pulp Literature.

$\mathcal{D}$ESDEMONE

Without delving into the precise nature of my profession, I am known for my stealth. No man or woman who walks the Earth may see me unless I wish.

But there was one Christmas Eve long ago, when I came upon a house buried by tall drifts of trackless snow. No one had come or gone in days.

I entered through a dormer window and shivered. The home inside felt colder than out. Indeed, it was a tomb. It possessed a mournful hush that strained, as if it had been noisy a few moments before.

I crept towards the stairs but then heard scraping from below. I froze. A man's voice called through a bedroom door. "Who goes there?"

The sound of a drawer slowly, even carefully, closing cut through the dark.

The man repeated, "Who goes there?"

I backed into an alcove and melted into the shadows. The door swung open. The man turned his ear and probed for the source.

Behind him, I saw the faint outline of a woman and a boy

under the covers of the bed. I believe their quaking roused the man. He straightened up. He mastered his fear. In a reassuring tone, he declared, "See, my son, it is nothing."

The boy said, "No, Father, my sister is awake."

"No, your dear sister sleeps."

The father stepped back into the room and shut the door. The mother began to sob. When she went quiet, I continued downstairs.

In a corner of the parlour stood a tree decorated with strings of popcorn, candy canes, and ball ornaments. On one branch, there sat a photocard of the boy and his sister.

I heard a knock. A draft swept by. A chill went down my spine. The floorboards creaked. Someone approached. Again I slipped into the shadows.

In the murk of the hall, a figure skulked, small footsteps coming closer and closer. A little girl emerged. She had raven hair and a white Chantilly dress. She knelt to the carpet and began to crawl, her locks falling, dragging on the floor. She groped under and behind the furniture and bookcases, searching for something. She bumped into a table. A small vase smashed.

"Who goes there?" called the voice from upstairs.

Its despair made my heart tighten. The girl ignored her father and continued her nocturnal hunt until her eyes fell on me. She squinted. "Is that really you?"

I summoned all my skill to fall beyond her perception, but she stood up and dusted her knees. "My friends at school said you were not real. But I knew."

I stepped from the wall, confused. "How do you, little girl, see me? No man or woman who walks this Earth may see me unless I wish."

The answer came when she threw her arms around my waist.

She was thin, frail, her substance as delicate as frost, her touch pure ice. From the folds of my deerskin coat, she muttered, "I cannot sleep."

"What is your name, dear child?"

"Desdemone."

"Desdemone, if I grant you a final gift, will you sleep?"

She pulled away from me. She whispered, "There is no gift for me to wish for."

"Nonsense. Name your wish, and I shall grant it."

Her lips trembled. A tear fell from her cheek. "The gift I want you have already given me. His name is Foster Theodore, and I cannot find Foster anymore."

The child began to wail. Her keening cut. The man called, pleaded from upstairs, "Please, please, who goes there?"

I scooped the wee thing in my arms. "Now, now. The fate of every toy that once sat beneath a tree is known to me."

I carried Desdemone up the stairs, past the bedroom to the end of the hall, to the study. I lifted her so she could reach a high shelf. She found a box and opened it.

"Foster!"

In a square of moonlight, she danced with her teddy bear.

The bedroom door banged. The father stormed towards the study. Desdemone and I slipped behind a curtain of black. Foster lay limp on the floor.

The father stopped and stared. He picked up the bear. He moaned and clung to it. "Is this why we suffer so? I hoard a token of my daughter that was not mine to keep?"

Only the night answered.

The father, treasured toy in hand, donned his coat. From the shed, he grabbed a pick and spade. He struggled through the deep snow until he came to the family burial plot. He bent over a lonely stone and beneath the cold stars broke the earth and ice. The man buried Foster Theodore where Desdemone lay.

Desdemone grabbed my hand and yawned. "Father Christmas, I will sleep and not wake?"

"Yes, Desdemone."

"But dawn, dawn will come?"

"Always, Desdemone."

"Then I say to you, Merry Christmas."

Before I could reply, Desdemone was gone.

FEATURE INTERVIEW

JJ Lee

Pulp Literature: *'Desdemone' moves between the eerie, the heartbreaking, and the hopeful. What first set you on the trail of this story of Father Christmas and a ghost girl?*

JJ Lee: I've been pursuing two goals. One is to write something as wonderful as 'The Shepherd' by Frederick Forsyth. I listen to the CBC Radio version every year, and five years ago I took a stab at writing my own Christmas Eve ghost story. And it's been my good fortune that CBC lets me read one every holiday season. 'Desdemone' in particular was my shot at writing a modern 'A Visit from St Nicholas' (aka 'Twas the Night Before Christmas'). It actually started as a poem but it wasn't very good. My writing group tore it apart. But I loved Desdemone so much, I had to rewrite it as a short, short story.

PL: *'Desdemone' aired on CBC Radio One on December 23, 2016. What is it like, reading your words aloud to an audience you can't see? How does the different medium affect the story and its creation?*

JJL: I write for speech as a general rule. I sometimes wonder if the way I read — which is pretty okay, because I was a broadcaster and I'm a natural ham — sells the story, whereas the words on paper may not. All I know is I can't read it aloud without choking up. But

I'm not sure if it touches the reader the same way. Try reading it to your family and let me know!

PL: *You've written and read aloud other ghostly Christmas tales. What is it about this combination that so draws you?*

JJL: It gets me in the mood for the season. It's not Christmas unless I write about lost children with broken hearts. I also think it reaches people who are, during the holidays, listening to the radio alone. I think about them a lot when I write these stories. And reading aloud, that's about gathering people together for a communal experience. It means a lot to me.

PL: *As an artist and a storyteller, how do these two approaches inform your work? Do you see the story behind a scene worked out in pen or pastels? Do your characters appear as character sketches before a word is written?*

JJL: I doodle after I write, but mostly the stories are little puzzles. They're worked out through writing and mental grinding. I simply don't know who is the ghost in my stories until I finish a draft, and even then it can switch. I'm a big believer in creation through discovery. Following a plot can become too mechanical, and the story becomes a map of plot waypoints. A surprised writer makes for a surprised reader, I say.

WE COME BACK DIFFERENT *Part 1*

AJ Odasso

AJ Odasso *is the author of three award-nominated poetry collections* (Lost Books *and* The Dishonesty of Dreams, *from Flipped-Eye Publishing;* Things Being What They Are, *unpublished and shortlisted for the Sexton Prize) as well as a handful of short stories. She serves as Senior Poetry Editor at* Strange Horizons *magazine. You can find her at twitter.com/ajodasso.*

$\mathcal{W}$E COME BACK DIFFERENT

PART I

3 June 18——
St George's, Bermuda

My dearest Tess,

In spite of the disagreeable circumstances under which we last parted, I hope that this letter finds you well. It will cheer you to know that your father's health is much improved since you left for Scotland this spring. He delights in your single-minded love of study, and his desire is that you should make as fine a scholar as your mother. But I must caution you, my love, to remember that there are pleasures in this world that do not concern anatomy, chemistry, or engineering. My ever-troublesome charge — Trevor is growing! — has found an expedient use for your old laboratory goggles. Your brother has taken to packing them for our jaunts to Horseshoe Bay. He has mastered the art of holding his breath underwater, during which time he is content, from behind glass through which you once squinted at dissections, to observe parrot fish the size of soup tureens.

Regarding our falling-out, I am not inclined to continue in such unseemly avoidance — for you have said that what you admire most is my forthrightness, and I hope I have not been foolish in treasuring your honesty. Do not take your wealth for granted: had my mother been rich, she would have wished for me an education as fine as yours. I understand that the completion of your degree is essential; I want nothing more than for you to perfect your skill in the sciences. All I ask in return is that you do not write off my fancies, for poetry and politics are equal to the task of improving humankind. Furthermore, I remain steadfast in my opinion that you have done poorly by Trevor. His musical talent continues to flourish, and although you set little stock by the performance he had so carefully prepared for your departure, he believes firmly that you are the cleverest, kindest creature ever to walk the earth. Write to him, Tess. He misses you.

For my part, I pass endless days in pursuit of Trevor and in seeing to your father's welfare. Although he is more sanguine than you will remember, his memory declines. For each time that he recognizes me, he supposes me to be your mother at least twice. I cannot persist in this sad affair without reassurance of your support — surely you may find the time to write more than once a month, so that my spirits might be lifted! I can take only so much solace in Trevor's compositions and in discovering which of your father's favourite strays has lately hidden her kittens amidst the banana trees and knee-high weeds in the garden. Artemis has dropped her first litter.

This corner of the world is monotonous, my darling. Be brilliant, and be well.

Ever yours,
Amelia

*   *   *

12 June 18 —
St Andrews, Scotland

Sweet Amelia,

This correspondence may reach your shores by sea rather than by air, much to my annoyance. The pilots' strike cannot continue indefinitely, so why not apply your political acumen to that when next you submit a column to *The Trans-Atlantic Weekly*? Several of the faculty here are ardent followers of your rambling yet sagacious wit. Perhaps it will earn you a scholarship.

Please do not think that I have not taken to heart the contents of your letter, but I must report a strange occurrence that has lately beset *my* corner of the world. Lansdowne, my tutor, has been ardently in favour of my chosen discipline — that is, the repair and replacement of organs and other such vital tissue through methods of hermetically sealed replacements, etc. I will not attempt another description of these devices' components, nor of the fusion by which they run in perpetuity. You, lively and insightful, must populate this world with wonders, whereas I, eternally brooding, must endeavour to unlock the causes of its unhappiest misfortunes and to repair them if I am able.

The occurrence of which I speak centres on one such misfortune, Amelia — the gravest of them all, I fear, to which none of us are immune. The body of a young woman washed ashore on the West Sands just over a week ago. My employment as liaison between the university laboratories and the local mortuary ensured my presence on the scene; I had the unfortunate task of interviewing the elderly gentleman who discovered the poor girl. He had hardly imagined his morning stroll would be thus ruined, and he could hardly bring himself to look upon me, I think, because he could easily imagine me in place of the corpse. I felt sorry for him.

It would have amazed you to see her. Pale skin, faintly blue beneath a wash of sand and sea water—so different from you, my Indian beauty, and from myself, wild-haired and brown-skinned with no hope of sorting out whence it has all emerged from my ancestors' trysts. She faced the sky, grey eyes wide, scarcely three hours dead (or so my reckoning would have it). You are the poet, yet I could not help but fancy the dark ribbons of her hair resembled endless, rippled strands of kelp. I closed her eyes and rolled her onto her side, folded up her limbs like those of a sleeping child.

We have employed the time since making ceaseless enquiries as to her origins. There have been no reports of missing persons matching her appearance, much less her age and sex. We have taken great pains to preserve her with minimal intervention; this art has long been a prized accomplishment of our institution. If this fair soul should remain unknown, I have pressed upon Lansdowne to ensure that she might remain with us as a subject. My research has thus far concerned the inner workings of disparate parts, but I am eager that I should begin to apply my findings, as it were, to the whole. A specimen so well preserved would be of great advantage.

I had not intended for this letter to dwell on matters you find macabre, my love, but at present this endeavour is the heart of my existence. I tire of precision-cut gears and steam burns to my fingertips as the only fruits of my labours. I must discover whether these devices work.

Fondly,
Tess

*   *   *

21 June 18—
Hamilton, Bermuda

Dear Tess,

We have situated ourselves in the townhouse for the time being, as your father has got it into his head that Trevor should audition for a violin teacher here in the city. Your brother has wearied of the visiting tutor in St George's, and, he is certain, can learn nothing more from him. Would that I had known my own mind so confidently from the age of ten! I might have been leagues away from this place by now, perhaps in Britain or France, or even in the Americas. If only you would take me with you, Tess, when next you return—Annabel Copeland's boy, Gareth, has been a great help at the villa. He is fond of your brother, and he would gladly take my place.

I find it troubling that you seem to take a kind of pleasure in this young woman's untimely death. I trust that there was at least a memorial service held in her honour before the scalpels descended. The first letter I have had from you in a full three months, and it was full of nightmares. Your constitution is strong indeed. I would not have handled that ghastly scene with such grace.

Promise me this, my Tess, if you can promise me nothing else: let no disrespect come to her. Should she be conveyed into your care for the furthering of your work, please remember that she once breathed, laughed, and spoke. Had a family, perhaps even a lover. Had a *name*.

Your father's memory does not fail him as frequently here as it fails him at home. He has been reunited with dear old friends, with whom he spends his evenings playing cards. Whereas I, too, find Hamilton enjoyable, I cannot help but recall that it bores you. Do you remember our sojourns in Par-la-Ville, your fascination with the lush greenery and the crumbling walls? I have only Trevor for companionship now. Although I love your brother dearly, he is no replacement.

Faithfully,
Amelia

✽   ✽   ✽

28 June 18 —
St. Andrews

Dear Amelia,

The pilots' strike has been resolved and a wages increase is under negotiation. I am continually surprised that you have not thought to protest with them; your voice would do as much good in the streets as it does in print. I sense that you feel a lack of purpose at present, and it pains me. If Gareth is as willing to take your place as you say he is, perhaps you ought to employ more of your time outside my father's household. As he is presently in high spirits and usefully occupied, and the family plans to remain in Hamilton for some time, perhaps you might contact local organizations regarding volunteer work. I trust that your monthly salary is still sufficient.

You will be pleased to know that the girl has been assigned to me for research purposes, and that due ceremony has been performed. Those of us attending to matters of forensics are not so heartless as you paint us. Regarding the matter of family, we have exhausted every avenue in the search for her origins. A name, however, we can provide her with, as is standard practice. I thought instantly of the wistful Greek legend of which you have always been so fond. Therefore, her name is Halcyon, in memory of her happier days amongst the living.

As for the scalpels, her flesh yielded as if made to the purpose. I made the first incision as swiftly and mercifully as I could. Her organs weighed and laid out were a sight of curious beauty, and these have been allotted to sundry of my colleagues. To me, they are useless refuse, the very broken pieces of machinery that I will, in weeks to come, replace. I have already mastered each and every last of their particular functions. I have only to replicate and install them.

She looks so peaceful in her sleep, Amelia. Please rest well in yours.

Thinking of you,
Tess

✻   ✻   ✻

Dear Tess,

Finish this project, discover whatever it is you must discover, and come back to us as soon as you can. Your father asks me almost daily why you have not written to him. I know the passion you bear for your work, but I fear for your well-being. She is not sleeping, my love; she is dead, whereas I am alive and waiting. Why must you persist in this feverish determination? I would call it *obsession*, but I am loath to think you might succumb.

Trevor is pleased with his new teacher. Master Dujon feels that he may be ready to play with the orchestra in a year or two, possibly sooner. I would not want him to rush, but he takes after his older sister: brash, eager, and impossible. Why have you not written to him? He would like me to inform you that Jacob Shillingford has agreed to take him and your father on a whale-watching expedition a week from tomorrow. He is tiring of your goggles and of holding his breath.

I have sent enquiries to several organizations, as per your suggestion. However, I cannot help but think that my time is better spent with your father and your brother until such time as I might accompany you to places far from this miserable backwater. It would not seem such a prison, Tess, if you were here. We might think of marriage, you with your science and I with my words.

Halcyon is dead; please remember that. But I am glad you

have given her a name. Report your findings to me as soon as you are able, and give her a fine burial at the last.

Yours in hope,
Amelia

✳   ✳   ✳

29 June

00.45

—Tracheal bruising and some burst alveoli. Strangled? No broken bones or torn muscles.

—Possible outcomes: damaged tissue may begin to repair itself. Other cellular regeneration.

—Desired outcomes: breathing & reflexes when induced. Circulation, as no blood was lost.

1 July

02.34

—Frightened a first-year student in the corridor. Someone told him it was haunted down here.

—Have begun work on heart-halves. Told the first-year he is definitely not allowed to watch.

10 July

01.29

—Frontispiece engraved w/ garnet-eyed swallow & my initials. If the examiners object, it will hardly cost me more than a few marks. Lansdowne says to check my damned pride.

12 July

15.35

—Reaction initiated; heart-halves sealed. *Agni*, Amelia would call it. Once left twenty-four hours to stabilize, will begin full installation of other completed organs. Dental work to pass the time.

19.27

—Brain stem prepared; incisions closed. External reactor and filaments in working order.

—Final inspection: all sutures have held, no damages beyond those noted on 29/6.

19.32

—Reaction initiated.

*   *   *

FOR THE URGENT ATTN. OF:
Ms Tesla Barnes
Dept of Forensics & Medical Technology
St Andrews, Scotland

FROM THE SENDER:
Ms Amelia Kingston
c/o The Barnes Estate
St George's, Bermuda

ON THIS DAY OF:
12 July 18 —

MESSAGE AS DICTATED:

Your father and Trevor are lost at sea.
Come home at once.

§

To be continued in *Pulp Literature* Issue 18, Spring 2018.

SEA CHANGES

Matilda Berke

Matilda Berke has been recognized by YoungArts, the Scholastic Art & Writing Awards, the LA Tomorrow Prize, the Molotov Cocktail's Shadow Award, and the LA Youth Poet Laureate competition, among others. She will be double majoring in English and Economics at Wellesley College. In her free time, she hopes to take up sailing and to read as many books as possible. Find more of her writing at Pedestal Magazine, Up the Staircase Quarterly, and matildaberke.weebly.com.

Sea Changes

So much mud on the new day. I am standing
with my head wet & your blue coat, both

slick as sidewalk forget-me-nots. Consider
all this a chorus. Fold
a newspaper boat in each riptide named

for our nation, for the etchings
in sand & unbloomed pavement.
You don't know it yet, but these

are the steps you will marry on. & these,
the champagne flutes filled with good clean rain

& here I will sit and wait.

~

There is a story on the islands
where a seal-girl comes to land

Sea Changes

& sheds her skin for a chance at genesis.
We were formed in the image of floating. & still,
I swam in the public pool so long I swore

my palms grew webs. You couldn't know
of midsummer tiles behind your chest & key,
of begging for birth in reverse. A lonesome

seadog with a book of Celtic myths.
I haven't seen the ocean since.

~

As a vessel vanishes, it goes in pieces.
Timber folding inwards, kindly. True mercy

bids it be this way. Leaving the sky no less
serene, no ship-shaped hole in the horizon.

We could be built like that, plank by plank
by plank. Only vaguely aware of missing.

DEVONIAN

Emily Osborne

Emily Osborne *is a researcher, translator, and poet living in British Columbia, Canada. She earned a PhD in Old Norse-Icelandic literature from the University of Cambridge and recently held a postdoctoral fellowship in medieval literature and linguistics at the University of British Columbia. She has taught mediaeval literature and poetics at Cambridge and UBC and published several scholarly articles. Her poetry has appeared in* The Literary Review of Canada *and* Symposium, *and she was runner-up for Eyewear Publishing's first Fortnight Prize. Emily has also published translations of Old English and Old Norse poetry in academic journals and books.*

DEVONIAN

Rocks older by zoic-eras, sophomoric and slick
with mosses and molluscs. A climate viscid
with early tetrapods, colossal flora.

Strata tempera, when insects innovated slowly
in Gondwana, when amphibian yolks
in Euramerica puddled in backwaters;
little gold auras becoming tadpoles
with a stroke, chromatic flecks
in the billions-big biota.

Small fauna, relics glassed in exhibits.
Crushed by calcite or resin-gummed,
skeletons that experts gesso
with muscle. Scales and tones guessed
by palaeontologists, chiming with dyes
in art rooms nearby.
Pedantic plaques suggest Devonian
palettes were narrow, when oceans
lassoed land, impassable,
and flashiness was risky in the greater hunger.

Perhaps. Shrouded by fronds,
proto-chameleons mingled in malachite mattes,
or varnished their backs to fascinate mates,
cloning an indigo spectrum, spawning
thousandfold replicas.

Museum-goers are titillated by halos of rust
and rarity, the crumble of a mother-and-child.
Brushes that recovered ancient bodies, icons
once so common one might string
their slight bones on a rosary.

THE BRIDGEWATER CANAL MYSTERY

Mel Anastasiou

In this fifth adventure in the Hertfordshire Pub Mystery series, Spencer Stevens tries to keep sober and afloat now that his long-lost true love Holly has re-entered his sphere. An increasingly demanding and difficult pub rebuild, troubles with long-distance love, and a trip back in time to solve a mystery involving treason and the murder of a redcoat soldier have Spencer Stevens wondering just how far he must travel before he gets a second chance at happiness and love.

Mel Anastasiou *is the author of* Stella Ryman and the Fairmount Manor Mysteries *(Pulp Literature Press, 2016)*, The Extra, A Monument Studios Mystery, *a growing number of novellas featuring Stella Ryman and Spencer Stevens, and several writing guides, including PLP's* The Writer's Boon Companion: Thirty Days Towards an Extraordinary Volume. *You're invited to follow her at melanastasiou.wordpress.com.*

The Bridgewater Canal Mystery

Chapter One

Summer is sometimes more an elusive hope than an actual season in the UK, but this June left no doubt in my mind that the glorious time of year was upon us. I believe every one of the motley band that gathered daily to fix up my not-quite-derelict Seven Swans public house — two DIY amateurs and a lone professional — felt the same about sunshine. When it actually shows up for the party, there's nothing like summer in Britain.

Which didn't mean it wouldn't rain. Therefore, the paint cans, brushes, white spirit, hammers, pointing trowels, and other paraphernalia that our elderly and highly competent builder Stan had suggested I purchase were well covered with a waterproof tarpaulin.

My friend-who-ran-off-with-my-wife Byron and I stopped beside Stan in the pub doorway. I had my phone out to show Byron the picture my long-lost love Holly had mailed me. In this, a more recent picture of herself, she was seated at a restaurant table by the sea. It reminded me of the picture I carried of her in my pocket for forty years. She no longer looked twenty, of course, but she was still lovely. She was Holly. Married to Morgan Odell. I believed, on no evidence but the expression of sorrow in her eyes, that she was unhappily married. "I can't have that," I told Byron. "Not for Holly."

Stan set his Guinness aside. "Lucky thing all your paint is hidden from view."

I had never seen old Stan abandon half a Guinness before. If I'd had any money at all, I'd have bet against it, no matter the odds and my overdraft. "Are you ailing for something, Stan?"

"Illness can't get a firm grasp on me, son. Now, I'm going to need you to bear up under the news I'm about to give you."

"All right." I glanced up. "Look, here's Eustace coming down the hill at last. Who's that with him?" A young fellow, it appeared to be, who steadied the much older Eustace when he stumbled on the path leading towards us.

"Exactly why we had to hide the paint." Stan squeezed my arm comfortingly. "That there is Eustace's nephew Cedric, the inspector of Grade II-listed buildings."

"You mean the one who tells me what kind of paint and wood I'm allowed to use?"

"Got it in one."

"Oh, gosh." The last thing I wanted was an inspection of the Seven Swans just now. Eustace had warned me. "Byron, find us glasses and some fizzy water."

"I wouldn't know it by sight," Byron said lazily. "You'd better go."

I waited by the doorway to the Seven Swans, feeling like a publican — for the first time in my days here beside the Bridgewater Canal — about to show my first customer around.

Cedric wore heavy boots and was as efficient as his uncle Eustace was convivial. He nosed around the outside of the pub, paying attention to the brickwork and the area I had myself painted before Stan informed me that Tudor-era pubs by law had to be painted with Tudor-era paint, which they don't sell at Costco, not even in the UK.

Cedric asked what the fresh paint was about, and Eustace said sententiously that it must have been vandals.

"I'm sure." Cedric looked at me suspiciously. He entered the building. Stan, Eustace, Byron, and I stood about outside. I felt like a hoodlum and looked, I'm sure, like a DIY buffoon, while a lot of knocking of fists and boots on the unfinished 1980s plywood bar and fittings sounded from within. I sucked my lip and wished I could finish Stan's Guinness without falling back into the life of a raging alcoholic. I just wanted to run my pub and invite my old girlfriend Holly to visit. Without her husband.

At last Cedric emerged. "Well, the interior appears to have been designed by a village madman and built by his cat. Now for the bad news."

Byron said, "You don't like to cushion the good news, do you, old boy?"

"How can that be the good news?" I asked.

"Just hold on," Eustace said.

"And brace yourselves," Stan suggested, "because you're about to be treated to a lot of chemistry."

"The bad news," Cedric continued patiently, "is that a Grade II-listed building has to be renovated like-for-like. That is, if the paint on there now is Edwardian, for example, you have to paint it with the type of paint Edwardians used, and in that particular colour. Or, if rotted woodwork dates from medieval times, you have to find medieval bits of wood to fix it with. It can get pricey, but it must be done correctly."

We all moved a little to block the tarp-covered cans of paint I'd bought on sale.

Stan said, "Don't look so gloomy, Spencer, tomorrow is a new day."

"I'm not gloomy, I just don't know how to get Tudor-era paint."

Cedric said, "I said like-for-like. This pub was painted as recently as 1870. You just need Victorian era paint."

"Got some of that in me back pocket," Stan joked.

"I like a bit of original Georgian whitewash on my garden fence," Eustace added.

Cedric laughed like the good nephew he no doubt was. "And the interior fittings are modern, by which I mean forty years old, so you can do as you like inside, within the context of the original design, without having to resort to finding wood, for example, from a particular age. Unless you want to, of course."

"How long will it take, in your experience?" I asked. "To fix up the Seven Swans and get a new licence? You must have seen a lot of pub renovations."

Cedric said, "Not long, really, with the four of you working. A year, maybe two."

He led the way into the pub to show them the fittings within and to explain just why they were unfit and could never be fit again. I felt a bit like the fittings, and hung back on my own. I crossed the canal by the lock and stood on the verge of the River Bulbourne where it ran parallel to the canal. I gazed at my pub. "You know what?" I asked the Seven Swans. "If you had to be derelict, why not go all the way, and be demolished? Razed to the ground. And then I'd be the lucky one, because I'd never have seen you."

In the silence that followed I felt ashamed of my words, so I added, "Sorry. I'm just in a bad mood, I guess. I take it back."

The next second, the Seven Swans winked out of existence, leaving on the rocky ground just a smudge of charcoal where the old fireplace had stood and a foundation shape drawn with dirty rock and mortar.

CHAPTER TWO

The canal still flowed, and the River Bulbourne still ran close beside it. I stared at the spot where my pub had stood. This feeling of loss and error was like gazing upon Holly's picture across the decades and knowing that the world had given me some bad breaks but nothing like the ones I had brought upon myself: time lost, breaks in acquaintance, breaks of trust. I had long ago abandoned Holly, and now I felt I had somehow done the same to the Seven Swans.

The unfairness of it, on top of Cedric's diagnosis (and where were Cedric, Eustace, Stan, and Byron anyway, now that the pub was gone?) was like an unmerited blow to my midsection. How could I possibly rebuild it from the ground upwards? I had my memories of the Seven Swans, but no plans or sketches. I would have to work them out myself, somehow. It would take years to rebuild, given the small reno funds my ex-wife's parents had allotted for its reconstruction.

Was I ready to do whatever it took to bring back the Seven Swans? As I asked myself the question, the pub reappeared in its place upon its old foundations. The late spring sunshine showed up clearly every battered brick, all the crumbled pointing, and even the red veins in the petals of the rose that grew up beside by the back door.

I took a step towards the back door where the rose grew, a sign that the Seven Swans was returning to life, beauty, and service. Another step, and the place vanished again. I waited. The spot where the pub stood remained bare. Gone, just like the forty years that I might have spent with Holly.

I knelt and looked closely at the crumbled foundations. Hallucination was playing on me, and it seemed unfair to the highest degree that I should be seeing visions without touching a drop of alcohol. I double-checked my memory: had I slipped out of old habit and downed a pint of strong ale or a swift snifter of scotch? I had not, except in my dreams. But now I wanted some, and I couldn't have it.

No wonder despair is marked a perilous fault in a man. I felt as if my heart would stop beating if I didn't take a drink. I sat down hard on the canal's edge. Safely on land, with a mouth dry as desert rock, I felt as if I were drowning.

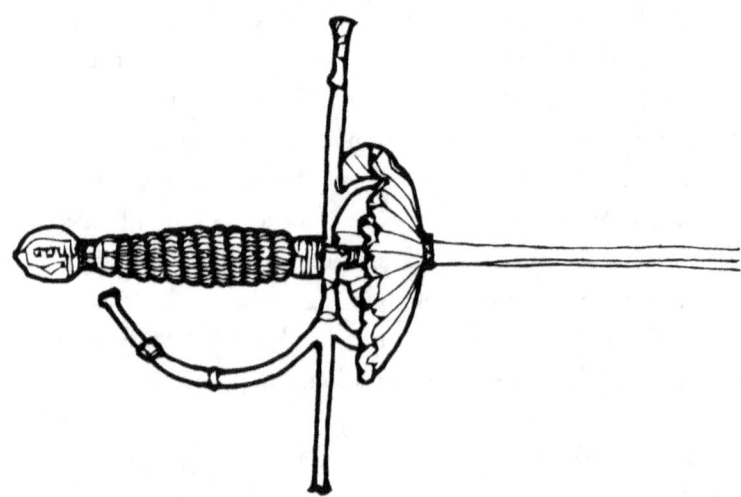

CHAPTER THREE

April 16, 1758

It is not yet ten o'clock of the morning as the cold river water closes over my head and the Seven Swans pub drifts out of view. I'm sorry to say that my first fear is for my good new wig, for which I have not yet paid. The river takes it, tugging it away from my head as I flail about in my velvets, also newly purchased for service to the Duke of Bridgewater. My second worry is for my life, because death by drowning is famously one of the less comfortable ways to go, and furthermore, it leaves a most pathetic corpse behind for others to gaze upon, including the fellow who pushed me in. All in all, I am in a sorry state, but as I swim in the brown water with the sticklebacks of the River Bulbourne, the light-filled bubbles sing to me, and I look up at the delicate skating of water spiders across the surface. This brings memories of childhood days not so very long ago, when I splashed with long-lost Blanche in this same river, along with Rickard Mudd, who by strange coincidence is the same fellow who pushed me off the river's edge just now, shouting that he'd lost his leg thirteen years ago today, cut off by the Scots in war, and therefore the least I ought to do is obey his wishes.

I kick at the rocky river bottom. Poor Rickard. I wish him happy, even though he pushed me into the river. When he, Blanche, and I were very young, thirteen years ago, he and I vied for her love, and lost, not to each other, but to Bonnie Prince

Charlie, warrior and cad. Blanche, a Hertfordshire lass and publican's daughter, hadn't a drop of French or Scottish blood in her, but tales of the Stuart Pretender's glories drew her away to be near him. And Rickard had followed her, but properly, on our British king's side, hoping to win back, or at least to capture Blanche and bring her home, no doubt kicking and biting, from behind the rebels' lines. But hope availed nothing, back in '45, not for the Pretender prince who licked his wounds and retired to France, his drink, and his married mistress. And not for Rickard Mudd, who at fifteen years of age lost a leg fighting that rebellion. Rickard was even worse off, as he only had drink to return to.

I gaze upwards through the few feet of limpid river water that separate me from the surface. The foamy bubbles around me rise and disappear. In this peaceful moment, the black paddle feet and white underpinnings of a Queen's Swan pass overhead. It's actually possible to die this way. I worry for what I ought to have thought of first: my master the Duke's letter of credit, which I must deliver into the right hands. It is folded and tucked firmly inside the lining of my jacket, and I can't perish before I deliver it. As a child I swam naked and freely, whist now I'm weighted down by my velvet jacket and the rest of the heavy, good-quality clothing that a Duke's equerry wears. But when I stop thinking about drowning, and think about swimming instead, my old skills take over. I splash to the surface and make my way, hands and feet churning, towards the shore. The river is swollen with April rain, so the shallows bring me close to the little brick-paved yard out front of the Seven Swans. My horse, one of the Duke's mounts, eyes me placidly from its tether by the river's edge. I haul myself up onto all fours and onto my feet.

I find my wig plastered to the front of my coat, hooked onto the silk frog closures. I pull it free and wring it out with care.

Rickard is talking to himself somewhere around to the woodland side of the Seven Swans. I slosh that way in stocking feet to give him a piece of my mind. But as I round the pub corner I find that somebody else is already doing so. There before the side entrance, a county Justice of the Peace bristles with grey whiskers and the fury of a man dragged for no good reason away from his Sunday afternoon pipe. Sir Clement Redburn has Rickard by the frayed red collar of his old uniform, that of a foot soldier of "Butcher" Cumberland. The war is long over. However, Rickard still wears his red coat.

The Justice of the Peace is shaking him and calling him by his nickname, *Rickard Redcoat*, which no one ought to do to a fellow who is twenty-eight and lost his leg to war.

Both men have their backs to me, and indeed appear so angry that they might not have noticed my presence anyway. Rickard's crutch is losing purchase among the pebbles underfoot, and he holds himself upright on the leg that war spared.

Rickard says, "Go upstairs and see, sir, I beg you."

"Rascal, there is nobody in this public house but mice and spiders. The doors are locked, and dust sheets cover all the tables."

"Blanche must be upstairs. I followed her here," Rickard protests. "Blanche, a Frenchman, and an Irishman, I swear it. Blanche says the true Stuart king is coming. I would hunt down and kill Prince Charlie myself when he lands on English soil, but I think we would all rather see him hang."

Rickard sees Bonnie Prince Charlie behind every tree, but today is his first mention of Blanche's return. Could it be true, that she is back? Blanche is not the kind to write letters home, as

I have good reason to know. If she is back in Hertfordshire, she would certainly visit her parents' pub, for how would she know that they have sold the Seven Swans to the Duke of Bridgewater for his canal? And moved themselves earlier than expected to a timbered cottage in Abbot's Langley, for they are not here to receive their payment and give me the deed of ownership, for the Duke.

I say, "Rickard, you know as well as I do that Blanche lives in France now, to be near the Stuart Pretender to the throne."

Sir Clement loosens his grasp on Rickard. "Another of you? The whole town is talking about the Pretender as if he was in England yesterday. The war is long over. The whole story stinks like old fish and should be forgotten."

Rickard rights his crutch and squares his shoulders. "Thirteen years ago today we beat that Stuart scoundrel at Culloden, and now he's back."

"He's not back. He's never coming back." The Duke stares harder at me. "What, is that you, Spencer? The Duke will hear witness that I saw his equerry here, drenched like a cat in a water barrel. Why are you wet?"

Rickard Mudd was once my friend. "I fell in the river."

Rickard says, "I pushed him."

Sir Clement says, "I judge this an assault."

"It's just an old habit of ours, from when we were children, and then our famous rivalry," I explain, to lighten matters. "We loved the same girl, she followed Prince Charlie to war, and Rickard blames me for letting her. He went after her, and the Scots took his leg, and he blames me for that, too."

Rickard says, "No, I blame the Scots."

The Justice says, "There are no Scots around here."

"But Bonnie Prince Charlie is coming back to Britain, to claim his throne."

Sir Clement takes me some little ways aside. "This fellow's lost more intellect than leg."

"Sadly," I murmur back. "And so perhaps you might let this whole matter go, seeing as he lost so much in the King's service. I will speak to the Duke about your kindness to a crippled veteran."

"I can hear, you know," Rickard says.

The Justice's scowl deepens. "Rickard Mudd, you are not the only man here who has given service to the Crown." He unties his horse from the ring on the pub wall and mounts.

Rickard stands on his good leg and waves his crutch for attention. "It's because I love the King that I want you fellows to see what's inside the Seven Swans."

Whether he hears Rickard or not, the Justice rides away without a backward look.

Rickard tugs at my shoulder. "Come, help me upstairs."

"The Seven Swans is now the Duke's property." This is not quite true, since I still have the Duke's money in my pocket to pay for it. My velvets are sopping, and my boots feel more like overcooked cabbages than good leather, but wet or dry, I know my duty. "You will have to ask him before such a trespass."

Rickard laughs. "How many times did we climb in open windows when we were boys? We cared nothing for dukes back then."

"Go home, Rickard," I say, although I know what a hovel corner of a dastard inn he inhabits.

"I will, if only you will look upstairs. Blanche is here."

I look up at the window. "She is not, for she would be leaning out and laughing at us."

"True. But perhaps she's learned caution."

We exchange a glance. Such a change would be most unlikely.

Rickard asks, "Do you by any chance have the key to the place?"

"No." The owners are meant to hand the key to me with the deed of ownership, in exchange for the Duke's money.

"Then I will climb in by the window." Rickard moves in the swinging gait he's developed to hurry himself along with his crutch. We both know about the side window of the pub that only appears to be locked, for we helped Blanche break the latch when we were young. Rickard uses his crutch for purchase and pulls the window up. Even to me, a hale fellow only twenty-eight years old with both my legs, it seems a higher scramble than when we were thirteen or fourteen.

"Push me up," he says.

I squeeze the water out of my jacket tails, and with what courtesy I can manage, move him to one side. I clamber through the window. Once inside, among the furnishings with their dust coverings, I lean back outside. "What exactly am I looking for?"

"You're looking for Blanche."

"But you know what she said." *I won't come back unless with Bonnie Prince Charlie himself.*

"Spencer, go and look upstairs for something that you don't expect, but I do."

"Please don't be mysterious," I say.

"Someone, then. A particular personage. Hiding upstairs."

I recognize the set of his screwed-up, bitter features. There is only one man in the world that Rickard Redcoat makes this face about.

"Bonnie Prince Charlie is not upstairs in the Seven Swans public house," I say.

"Tell me that after you have searched it."

"And after that you will go home and let me return to the Duke's business."

I leave Rickard outside, pass by the public room, and mount the stairs to the living quarters up above. Blanche's parents have taken their furnishings with them to Abbot's Langley, I see. They have left their own room flawlessly neat and well swept. I wonder whether they would have cleaned it quite so well for the Duke if they knew he aimed to knock the whole place down to put the canal through to Birmingham.

I expect to find Blanche's old room in a similar state when I open her door, or at the very most the neat white bed, carven box for her clothing, and clothes hooks on the wall the way they were when I was young. What I do not expect is what I find: an empty room, but not as the pub owners would have left it, for their fittings were always plain. Now the walls are hung with yellow silk. A feather bed rests upon a large curtained bedstead, and all about are furnishings rich enough to please a king.

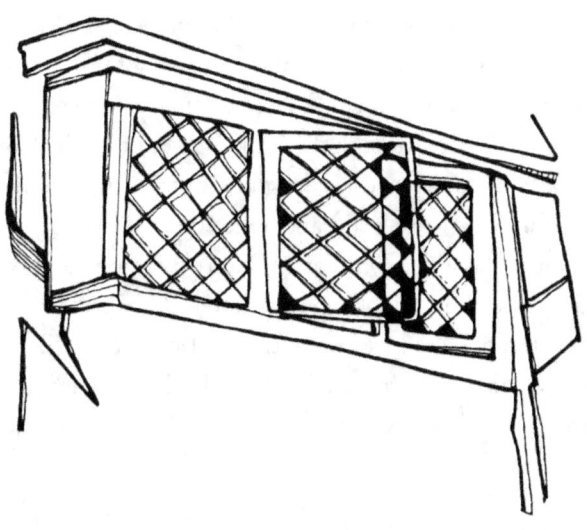

CHAPTER FOUR

I descend the stairs and make my way back to the window that lets out into the Seven Swans's yard. It might be that the Duke has furnished Blanche's old room, either for himself or for a friend. Who else has the money for such luxury? Not even Sir Clement, Justice of the Peace. It's beyond me why the Duke would want to stay in a riverside public house. But mine is not to guess at the Duke's motives. Mine is to make very sure that he never finds out that I haven't yet paid his money to the owners, which I was meant to do before noon today. The Duke is a good man, but fellows like me look to our steady employment and do not let our master down.

I close the door. I hurry downstairs. Rickard is gone, which is surprising but welcome, for I must make haste to Abbot's Langley to complete my purchase of the Seven Swans in the Duke's name. Out back, I untie from its tether ring the Duke's horse that is mine to use. I ride to Abbot's Langley and complete the job. Blanche's parents take the Duke's note of credit from me, and I casually ask after their daughter, but they have heard not a word from her since a letter and a nice bit of cheese arrived this past Christmastime from Paris. I don't mention the luxurious room I discovered in their public house. Far be it from me to confuse the poor old folk with talk of rich fittings. The Duke is paying a fair price for the land and buildings withal.

I'm nearly dry now. I'm grateful to be healthy and wish

Rickard were, too, and that he had two legs under him. No wonder he drinks. I vow to rekindle my friendship with him. It's never too late for a second chance, for him or for me. Perhaps I can help him make some kind of a life, for he was always good at his lessons, and there are London printers who will pay for the reminiscences of old soldiers, if they are bloody enough. I will ask the Duke, whose circle includes London aristocrats who pen poetry and even novels. Planning thus, I make my way on horseback along the lanes, carpeted with bluebells on every side, back to the Duke's Ashridge estate. I'm determined to reach my master with his deed of ownership, the twentieth thus acquired along the proposed canal route, before he sits down to his supper. The Duke's horse's hooves and church bells tolling round and fair combine in a hearty music. I count the tolls at twenty-eight, and then another twenty-eight, which is just my age, mine and Rickard's. I wonder who is dead at such a young age.

I find the Duke of Bridgewater working over plans for the canal at his desk in the great house's library. The clerestory windows admit the bright light of late afternoon from above, so that his wig shines white as Noah's dove in sight of land. My own wig is still damp from the river and smells like a wet dog just in from the rain. The Duke sets down his pen and pushes aside a sheaf of notes, with care not to brush the engineering drawings that Gilbert, his chief agent and engineer, has been bringing to him for the last year and more. These are designs for the canal that will link London to Birmingham in prosperity's name. The Seven Swans section of the river is a small link in the long chain of properties through which the canal will cut, running, just at the public house's point, parallel to the River Bulbourne. Hertfordshire and environs will be the wealthier for it, as will the Duke. What is good for him is good for all, myself included.

The Duke opens the deed of ownership and nods his thanks to me. "Are these former owners still content with the price?"

"They all but kissed me, sir."

He smiles. "A narrow escape. But I am sorry, Spencer. I should not joke when you've had bad news today."

I frown. *Bad news?* "It was more a surprise, sir, when I checked an upstairs bedroom at the Seven Swans ... "

He interrupts. "I mean your friend. Rickard Mudd."

"What's wrong?" I picture Rickard, struggling with the Justice of the Peace at the river's edge. "Has he been cast in gaol again?"

"Did you not hear the church bells ringing? Sit down." The Duke pulls a chair away from the wall for each of us. "Your friend is dead. I'm sorry."

"How can he be dead?" I hold tight to the chair arms. "Rickard is only twenty-eight." His injuries from the war?

"He drowned." The Duke rings a bell, and when his servant Jem appears, he asks for whisky and two tumblers. "Gilbert found him an hour ago, when he rode down to check the place before sending men to raze it to the ground. Your soldier friend was floating face down in the river next to the Seven Swans. Did you not hear the bells?"

He hands me a glass of Scotch whisky.

Afternoon sunlight brightens the rows of books around us. It occurs to me that although the Duke is younger than I, he has probably read many of them, and I have read none.

I can't bring myself to drink my whisky. "Rickard Mudd did not like anything from Scotland after the war, not even good whisky."

The Duke raises an eyebrow, and I remember that one of his cousins by marriage is Scottish.

I add, truthfully enough, "But I myself have nothing but friendly feelings for Scotland, now that they all keep the King's peace."

I drink to Rickard.

The Duke raises his glass with me. "Today is April sixteenth, is it not? Then the final battle was exactly thirteen years ago."

"So Rickard said." I drink again and feel warmer than I have since he pushed me into the river.

The Duke takes the empty tumbler from me. "Word goes 'round that Rickard Mudd took his own life."

"I don't think so, sir." I picture Rickard, still wearing the same red soldier's coat he'd worn in the war. Still broadcasting his loathing for Bonnie Prince Charlie Stuart. Still in love with Blanche. "If he were going to take his life, he'd have done it long ago. Could it not have been an accident?"

"It might, if he were able to stab himself twice before he fell into the river. Are you certain he would not kill himself, Spencer? Much rides on your answer."

Rickard's life has for twelve years been an example of terrible disrepair, and I suppose that he might have lost hope. But a man who loves sherry as much as Rickard will not intentionally depart this world for another. Whether he is being welcomed in Heaven, as I hope, or in Hell, he's not likely to be offered a drink.

I study the Duke's face. This is a good man, with a business-man's soul. Why does he care so much? Perhaps my old friend did the Duke a good turn once? Unlikely. The Duke of Bridgewater doesn't need soldiers, and he has his own drink.

"Sir, you didn't know my old friend Mudd well, did you?"

"Never met him." He gestures at the whisky bottle. I shake my head. "It seems most of the town, including our good Justice of the Peace Clement, does not believe Rickard Mudd was worth killing."

"Everybody knows that if Rickard had on him anything worth murdering for, he would have long since traded it speedily for sherry."

"Poor lad." The sentiment does not sound strange, although the Duke is younger than Rickard, and me, by a good six years. "Spencer, I trust your judgment, and I would like you to look into the matter."

"Find out what happened?"

"Yes."

"How Rickard died? You mean, investigate his killing?"

"His murder, yes."

"I see." This time I take the re-filled tumbler and drink. "But I am no lawyer, nor a soldier, either. I'm your equerry."

"You're an exceedingly good equerry, though." He pours himself another whisky. I've never seen him take three at once, not since a small farmer near the Gade Bridge dug in his heels and would not sell his land. "You are such an excellent equerry, for example, that when the owners of the pub outside which Rickard's body would soon be found were not there to accept my payment, you tracked them down and completed your mission."

I begin to see where logic is leading, and I would rather get there before he does. "Sir, if I had not completed the transaction for you, they would still own the land."

"You see clearly. If you hadn't done such admirable work for me, this murder would not have taken place on my property."

"And the case for building your canal, sir, is still being

considered by the Government." I stand. I empty my glass. I straighten my wig and shoot my cuffs. "I'll find the killer, sir."

I reach the library door when the Duke calls me back, one hand in the pocket of his coat. "I've two things for you, Spencer."

He pulls out a bit of parchment I recognize as one of his letters of credit, scans it, signs it, and blots it with care. "First, use this if need be. I find it's useful to wave about this kind of money. If you need small coins, you'll see my St Albans banker, and he'll set you right."

Wave it about? I take the curlicue-decorated parchment from him, and when I read the amount, my mouth drops. A person could start a whole new life with this kind of money. His trust in me warms me more than whisky.

The Duke says, "Sometimes the possibility of a large sum of money is worth more than coins in the hand."

"I'll return it uncashed," I vow.

"That would be very nice indeed," the Duke says dryly. "And just what I expect of you, Spencer. You're a good man. Do you know where you'll begin to find out how Rickard met his end?"

"Not really, sir. I'll think on it, though. I have a possible lead." More of an impossible lead: Rickard's rumour of Blanche's return with an Irishman and a Frenchman. I fold the letter of credit safely away.

The Duke rests one hand atop the engineering tomes beside the drawings on his desk. The stack of books is topped with a history of Riquet's canal in southern France. I recall the Duke telling me that Riquet was a tax collector who died before his canal opened, and that we as Englishmen might all build better and live longer than that.

"Spencer, here then is the second thing I mentioned. It is an idea that may be useful to you. Ask yourself, why now? What has changed, that Rickard should die at this particular moment?"

I frown. The answer to that question is the same as before: Blanche, an Irishman, and a Frenchman.

It occurs to me that when Rickard was alive and pushing me into the river, I disbelieved that Blanche had returned to Hertfordshire. Now that he was dead, I was almost certain that I would find her somewhere nearby. I check the light at the window. Dark approaches. I'm eager to leave and find Blanche, if she is here. For my master's sake.

The Duke lifts his hand from his books and turns his palm towards me. "One more thing, Spencer."

Three things, then. I bow.

"If you wish to continue your employment with me, you will not begin your investigations until morning."

I look up, startled. "Sorry, sir. I will brush my jacket properly and see to my wig."

"I don't care about your wig so much as your neck. You're an efficient fellow, and if there's a murderer loose, I'd rather you caught up with him in daylight. Goodnight, Spencer."

"Goodnight, sir."

I sleep in a small room high up in the Duke's Ashridge house. My bed has nothing like the silken splendour in Blanche's old room in the Seven Swans, but it's a good old bed, and I'm so tired that I fall asleep without drawing the obvious conclusion. But it hits me at the same moment that first light strikes through my casement window. I'm dressed and on horseback before anybody but the Duke's bakers are about.

I thunder down the hill, through the bluebell woods, towards the River Bulbourne, to reach the Seven Swans. The grass out back muffles the sound of hooves, and I pull up before we touch pebbles or brick. I loop my bridle around one of the Seven Swans's many tether rings and I'm in through the downstairs window, up the stairway to the second floor, and through the door to Blanche's old room before anybody has a chance to stir.

But the room is empty. All is in the same condition as the day before, when Rickard bade me look inside.

Or rather, almost the same condition. There is one important difference: the bed is in slight disarray. Somebody slept here. I look beside and underneath the bed for some proof—a stocking, a hairpin—that Blanche has been here. I find nothing but the imprint of a head upon this pillow: witness the dimple in the centre.

Is it possible that I would remember the scent of her hair? Thirteen years ago, she left me for Rickard, and she left Rickard for Bonnie Prince Charlie. My memory balks at such a span of changes and chronology. But I pick up the pillow anyway to test my memory and because I promised the Duke to investigate Rickard's death to the best of my abilities. And anyway, I still miss her.

I breathe deeply. The slip of cloth gives up its aroma. But it is not Blanche's particular bouquet. I sniff the silk cover again, to be certain. Feathers, of course, but also a familiar odour. I remove my wig and sniff inside its crown. My deduction is irrefutable: Blanche never slept in this bedding. Nor did any woman. I know the particular smell of glue that those of us who are gentlemen, or almost gentlemen, use to keep wigs in their proper place atop the crown of our heads. The man who slept here wore a wig.

CHAPTER FIVE

Now that I've revisited the luxurious room upstairs at the Seven Swans, and now that the sun has risen to slant through the rowans at the water's edge, I'm grateful for the Duke's horse. I need greater speed, because I'm searching for not one but two people: Blanche, and a man who wears a wig and enjoys a prince's bedding for his good sleep.

I have learned in my time as the Duke's equerry that when two tasks present themselves at once, it's best to complete the easier of the two first, and it sometimes follows that the more difficult endeavour untangles itself on its own. But I decide that as the Duke's man, I must take some trouble with my appearance. A St Albans barber combs and perfumes my wig, while the barber's daughter takes my outer clothing home to brush and steam the pile back into my velvets. As the barber shaves me, I ask him whether he's seen anything of Blanche, the publican's daughter, but he's new in town only ten years back and never met her. I tell him that she ran away to follow the rebels, and he nods as he scrapes beneath my chin. He says, "I hear tell the Young Pretender is on the move again." I straighten up at this news. The barber doesn't cut me, so I tip him well, for that and for his source of information regarding Bonnie Prince Charlie's unlikely advent.

The barber sends me to the Old Bell public house, further south along the river from the Seven Swans. The Old Bell has no part in the Duke's canal plans, as the Seven Swans does, and the company here shows up early and thirsty. I see Pearl, whom I know well from my youth, pouring pints at the bar. I make my way to her and buy a pint of the unassuming ale she serves. Tankard in hand, I drift from table to table, asking questions of those about the place and silently thanking the barber for such an excellent trail to follow. It's true the pub is buzzing with talk of Charles Stuart.

As one old fellow puts it, "I hear tell the Pretender is on the move again. The devil take him."

"Where do you hear all this?"

"I heard it over at the White Hart."

Twenty minutes later, over the roar of a wedding party in its final hours, I'm listening to an idle labourer tell his table, "They're saying Bonnie Prince Charlie thinks he'll take his crown. Will the Stuarts never learn?"

"Where did you hear about this new attempt?" I ask. "Is there an Irishman, a Frenchman?"

"An Irishman stopped by the Goat."

At the Goat, somebody has broken crockery inside the front door. I pick my way through it and discover that they've had more news. A boy who must have been a babe in arms when the Scots rose up tells me as one who knows, "The Old Pretender wants his son the Young Pretender to marry some new lady before he'll get him any more money to come back to England."

An even younger fellow says, "And Charlie Stuart won't marry until he gets the crown."

An old fellow adds, "They can argue all day as far as I'm concerned, so long as they do it in France."

I ask the two young ones where they heard all this, and they answer, "An Irishman. At the Old Bell."

When I arrive back at the Old Bell, where I started, a blacksmith at the first table is holding forth to all around him. "I hear the Prince has established himself in Hertfordshire, with a beautiful lady to be his wife. But I'm not having any of your nasty Stuarts. Remember the hanging judge, that handsome Jeffreys."

Roar of laughter. "Still handsome when he was hanged himself."

I ask, "Where do you hear all this?"

"The woman herself, gone upstairs with her footmen."

Pearl, whom I knew long ago, is at the bar, still as pretty as her namesake. She says, "You know, one of them men of hers is even fancier than she is."

"She? The beautiful lady?"

"Blanche. I think you know her. The publican's daughter, who ran away to war?"

"Why in the name of all the fishes in the sea did you not tell me this when I was first here, Pearl?" I ask. "You might have saved me a journey."

"You never asked me, and I never begged attention from a man in my life." Pearl lifts her chin. "Anyway, I never liked that Blanche. Too bad you and poor old Rickard never took your eyes off her back then to look around at some others I could mention."

"Sorry," I say.

"Certainly, you're the Duke's equerry now, and too far above me for a kiss out back of the kitchen. But you've been round the houses searching after what's right upstairs. So now I am repaid." She laughs.

I bow. "Pearl, you have your revenge. And I thank you for the help, as does the Duke."

"Oh, a fair likeness of a gentleman, aren't you?" Pearl says. "Off with you upstairs to see Blanche, my lad. Second room on your right."

I mount the stairway from the public room to the chambers above, planning all the while to approach Blanche, the Irishman, and the Frenchman in stealth. I wouldn't put it past Blanche to carry a knife in her belt, as she did when she went off to follow the war, and the two strange men would certainly carry arms. Naturally, I have never been one for listening at doors, but duty trumps honour today, for the Duke specifically instructed me to stay alive. Therefore, it is my intention to begin by eavesdropping on the three of them through their closed door.

Once I reach the landing at the top of the stairs, eavesdropping is not necessary, or even possible. A commotion of voices issues through the half-open door of the second room on my right, followed by the sound of metal upon metal. Steel upon steel. The thin shining sound that swords make when they meet, in fact. Two men shout in French. Those below in the bar room fall silent.

Never mind the Duke, or my safety. I fear now for Blanche.

I count to three outside Blanche's door, for calm and concentration.

One. I was taught thus by the Duke's fencing master in a moment of leisure, when he showed me a thing or two. But I don't have a sword, or any weapon at all except the Duke's letter of credit.

Two. The silence from below highlights the clatter of swords on the far side of the door. Britain battles regularly with the French and the Irish, and both are doughty foes.

Three.

Chapter Six

I kick the chamber door open with one boot and enter. Blanche stands in front of the window on the far side of the room, which is exactly large enough to hold two men with rapiers. The Irishman and the Frenchman are almost nose to nose, their small swords locked at each other's hilts. All I know is that when two men with swords find themselves thus, they are meant to break, step back, and attack each other again. I judge one man the Irishman by his ginger hair and unassuming trousers and jacket. The Frenchman facing him lacks a wig to cover his dark hair, but is otherwise well dressed. His velvets in fact are better than my own, and from top to toe he brings to mind the gorgeous fabrics I saw in Blanche's room in the Seven Swans. And that is quite a lot to register just now. For they turn and face me. Unlike the fencing master's blade, these are so sharp that I think a man might shave with them.

I call across the blades, "Blanche, are you quite all right?"

"Oh, hallo, Spencer, is that you?" Her lovely face lights up with the joy I remember from long ago at seeing me, a shining gaze that nearly makes me forget why I am here. She has not changed at all, I see, and neither, apparently, have I.

The two men, having ceased their loud and incomprehensible invective, turn their swords towards me. In the sudden silence that follows I hear a collective gasp at my back, and spin round to find the whole company from the pub below standing in the corridor outside Blanche's room, goose-necking at the scene inside. Some of these have swords at their sides, too. If a larger fight breaks out, Blanche and I, both unarmed, will be at the mercy of a lot of sharp metal in a small space. I straighten my velvet jacket, the silk frogs lined up efficiently down my centre. I turn to address the crowd behind me.

"The Duke of Bridgewater," I begin, "has named me his agent and equerry ... "

A voice from the back of the crowd calls, "But he ain't here, is he, Spencer?" It sounds like Pearl's voice to me.

"Clear off now, everybody," I say.

Somebody else says, "Why should Spencer get all the livelong fun?"

The Frenchman asks something about a *duc*, and the Irishman growls overtop his words.

Outside the room, the patrons of the Old Bell are grumbling and wearing unfriendly expressions. I draw myself up tall and try not to think of the two blades at my back. I pull out the Duke's letter of credit and wave it at them. "The Duke has priority here, as you can see by this direct commandment, and anyhow I am his agent. Clear away, all of you." I sincerely hope they can see the curling writing of an aristocratic hand, or at any rate, an aristocrat's secretary's aristocratic hand. Equally, I trust that most of the Bell's clients do not read.

"Read it to us, then," somebody says.

"I have no time to do so." This is true enough. I tuck the parchment away again. "I bid you with all courtesy to return downstairs."

Pearl laughs. "Oh, come on then. Let's have another round, shall we, and let old Spencer shut that door in the name of the Duke."

"Thank you, Pearl." I do so, and face Blanche and her two armed companions.

Gracefully, she introduces the Irishman as Connor, and the Frenchman as Monsieur de Principe-Carneton.

I ignore their swords as best I can. "Blanche, you once vowed that you'd never return without Bonnie Prince Charlie himself. I ask, not to be unkind, but for clarification."

Blanche laughs the way she used to laugh when I kissed her by the River Bulbourne, out of sight of her parents and the Seven Swans. "I choose not to clarify."

"Why are you gentlemen here? You, sir?" I address Connor.

"A man may travel."

This is the dourest Irishman I have ever met.

"And do you agree with Blanche's estimation of Charles Stuart?"

"Oh, I think that Charles Stuart is a bonnie lad, glorious leader, and king-over-the-sea, who should be king right here in jolly old England." Connor shrugs. "Or something similar."

"But you do know that if Charles Stuart sets foot in Britain, he'll be hanged, drawn, and quartered?"

Connor shrugs again. "Not up to me, is it?"

The Frenchman is speaking rapidly to Blanche in his native tongue. Blanche looks helpless and turns to me. "Monsieur de Principe-Carneton doesn't understand. And I don't really know the details."

I make an effort not to flinch under the man's black-browed gaze. "Sir, first they invite everybody to watch. Secondly, they half-hang the traitor, slice open the fellow's middle, pull out his insides, and let him dangle and die slowly."

"That's the worst punishment I've ever heard of." Blanche has turned pale.

"I believe it's meant to deter treason," I explain.

Connor chuckles. Monsieur de Principe-Carneton pulls out his sword again and threatens me.

Blanche makes him put the sword away. "Even worse things happen in France, Monsieur de Principe-Carneton."

"Not to me," he says, in heavily accented English.

"Now, there's a coincidence," Connor says dryly, "That's exactly what the Prince said thirteen years ago when he made his escape. He was disguised as a pretty girl, wasn't he, Blanche?"

"I helped to disguise him. I'd do it again."

"I'm sure it won't be *necessaire.*" Monsieur de Principe-Carneton glances at the doorway, dons an extraordinarily good coat covered with embroidery, and sets a wig on his head.

All this reminds me that Bonnie Prince Charlie is peripheral to my search for Rickard's killer. However, when I look at that wig of Monsieur de Principe-Carneton's, I feel as if I'm closing in on important information. I take a good look at his sword, and Connor's as well, to remind me of the Duke's caution not to get myself killed.

I turn back to Blanche. "Did you know, our old friend Rickard is dead? Which of you saw him killed, down by the River Bul-bourne at the Seven Swans?"

"None of us has been near there. Poor Rickard." Blanche comes over to me and pats my hand. "You must be sad to lose your old friend."

"Thank you. He was your friend, too, and more, in our younger days," I say. Either she is lying, or she was never at the Seven Swans and the River Bulbourne, where Rickard was killed. But I know, from his wig and splendid garments, who was. "Could I have a word with Monsieur de Principe-Carneton in confidence, please?"

"*Non*," Monsieur says. "Speak to the Irishman."

"Before I do, tell me why you were fighting Rickard yesterday."

"I was not."

Does he lie? How to know? "Then tell me why you were fighting the Irishman today."

"*Bof.* Because if there is no énémi about, I fight with friends." He reaches under the bed and pulls out a small calfskin bag.

I decide I'm not likely to get anything but more lies out of Monsieur de Principe-Carneton, especially as he and Blanche have begun hissing long strings of French at one another. The Frenchman indicates the door at my back with a jerk of his bewigged head. I vow silently not to let anybody leave this room until I learn the true circumstances of Rickard's death. As I am the only man here without a sword, I'm not certain how I'll stop them, but the Duke's letter of credit could once again come into play. I decide that I might get something useful out of Connor, if I can only convince him to talk to me.

Connor solves that problem for me by drawing me aside so that his back blocks the only door to the corridor. I check over my shoulder to make sure that all is the same with Blanche and Monsieur de Principe-Carneton. He is brandishing his calfskin bag and the two of them are speaking more speedily than a fly buzzes.

There's a rattle outside the window, and Connor raises his voice to speak overtop the noise. "You want to know about the room in the Seven Swans, don't you? You saw it. You know who it is meant for? I see from your face you've deduced it."

"I have. It is meant for Bonnie Prince Charlie, when he comes. And I've also reasoned out something else. You're not Irish. You're Scottish."

Connor throws back his head and laughs loudly. "A good guess."

"And, you've come to protect your master upon his return."

He puts a hand on the hilt of his sword. "That's dangerous talk, sir."

"I didn't say the Pretender has returned." I look over my shoulder at Monsieur de Principe-Carneton, who is leaning out the chamber's window, looking down. "I say he ought not to return. I have no love of Stuarts, but I like to see a man keep his insides inside him."

There's the sound of horses outside the window. Connor raises his voice again, as if to keep my attention on him and him alone. "I see I must tell you our little group's secret."

Out of the corner of my eye, I see movement. I look about for Monsieur de Principe-Carneton, and see only Blanche leaning out the window. Connor pulls me closer. "Blanche would kill me for telling you this, but she is no great lady in the Prince's circle as she claims."

"Did she say so?"

"Yes, to everybody. Not to you, because you're obviously a

man who is hard to fool. But the truth is that she does know Bonnie Prince Charlie, for she is his married mistress's chambermaid, and she sleeps across the foot of their bed. On the floor," he clarifies.

"Heavens. Is she quite safe?"

Connor grips my arm before I can turn to look at her. I hear the swish of skirts from behind me, towards the window.

"But I will tell you the whole truth, now," Connor continues, as a thump and a cry sound outside. "She heard Charles Stuart bemoaning his poor luck with the throne. She was certain that Britain must be tired of Hanover kings, and that he would be received as he once was. All he had to do was go and his people would welcome him, and then of course there was the matter of divorces."

It is quite clear to me that Monsieur de Principe-Carneton has climbed out the window and caught Blanche as she followed him. They have horses beneath the window of the Old Bell, and the two of them are about to make their escape. I know what I should do. But I ask, "What do divorces have to do with anything?"

"The Prince's mistress is a married woman. Blanche called out from her place at the foot of their bed that British kings, since Good King Hal, could divorce as they wished, and the Pope can do nothing to stop them. So his mistress could be divorced, they could marry at last, and be king and queen of England together."

I raise my eyebrows. "But that is codswallop."

"Indeed." Connor sighs. "But attractive codswallop to a man who would like to make an already-married lady his wife and queen. Certainly worth sending an envoy to England to see whether it is true. His mistress's English chambermaid, his "Irish" footman, and his second-best French valet. Blanche makes a luxurious room at the Seven Swans for the Prince to come to, but he never will come. Monsieur de Principe-Carneton enjoyed its comforts, though."

I turn. The chamber is empty, now, as I knew it would be. Outside I hear horse's hooves and the jangle of harness moving down the road that leads away from town.

Connor's mouth makes a straight line, and he puts his hand to his sword. But I'm not about to try to push past him, nor summon soldiers, nor chase the two down as they make their escape back to France. For now I know who killed Rickard, and why.

"You were fighting just now with Monsieur de Principe-Carneton, because he didn't want you to stay and be tried for killing Rickard. He thought you could get away cleanly."

Connor inclines his head. "I'm sorry. That mad redcoat was your friend. You know why I killed him, though, and it wasn't for the sake of Bonnie Prince Bloody Charlie."

"No. It was for Blanche." I pale to think of her, my dear Blanche, drawn and quartered for treason.

Connor is right. Even thirteen years afterwards, even in a completely hopeless cause, by spreading talk of Bonnie Prince Charlie's return, she was abetting our own King George's enemies. And the punishment for that is hanging, drawing, and quartering.

"Rickard would have told the whole world about Blanche and her talk of the Stuart Pretender, so you killed him. To save her." I close my eyes. When I open them again, Connor is holding out his sword to me in surrender.

"Arrest me, sir. In the name of the Duke. Or the King. As you like."

I gaze at him. The fellow's life is in my hands. I imagine handing Connor over to Sir Clement, who will swiftly lay charges of murder and treason. My stomach turns. I would make a very poor Justice of the Peace. But I find that I can make a difficult choice.

"Connor, let's be off."

He screws up his face. "You can't be serious, man. How can we go?"

I think of Blanche, beautiful and brave, and the smile she gave me when I first entered the room. Of the touch of her lips on my face, on one cheek and then the other, as the French greet each other. I think it speaks well of France that they do so.

"I don't believe Blanche should be a chambermaid anymore, do you?"

"Well, I sometimes think she'd make an excellent footman's wife. But then I imagine that might be a dangerous life for the footman."

"Good. I'll take my chance as it comes, then." I pat my coat, where the Duke's letter of credit is tucked away. "Must we go out the window?"

"Down the stairs," he says. "I've had enough excitement in the last two days to last me into my eventual old age, if any."

"We'll go together, then. France is not so bad a place to live in, would you say?"

"Not so much rain as you see here. But I warn you, Paris is thick with *ducs*. They're everywhere."

We descend the stairway together and take a tankard of ale with Pearl. At the last, as we take our leave to follow Blanche and the Frenchman to France, I hand Pearl the Duke's letter of credit to return to him.

It's a bit of a wrench to let it go when it might solve, as my master promised, so many problems. But it's the right thing to do. And anyhow, if there are as many *ducs* in Paris as Connor promises, a good equerry may always find honest employment.

CHAPTER SEVEN

Somebody was dragging me by both arms away from the water's edge. My shirt bunched up, and pebbles dug into my skin and dragged along with me. I looked upwards to the right, where Eustace had me by the wrist, the strain showing on his narrow, friendly features. Stan, stalwart, had my left arm. They dropped me with a grunt apiece, and I sat up, dripping wet from head to toe. "Was I in the canal?" I asked. I didn't hear their answer. My ears were full of water, and anyway my whole attention was upon the Seven Swans. It stood before us, sturdy and as complete as it had been this past month since I had taken occupation.

The Duke of Bridgewater hadn't knocked the old place down to put through his canal. He was indeed an excellent Duke. In fact, I'd never met a finer one.

Byron appeared in the doorway. "Swimming, Spencer? I wouldn't advise it for another month."

Stan corrected him. "If you knew what was in that water … But now's not the time, perhaps, to go into detail on that subject."

"If you have to fall in at all," Eustace said, "I recommend the river instead. It's dirty, of course, but not actually foul."

I thank them both.

Stan said, "We're going down the pub. Can we get you anything?"

"Pimms?" Byron suggested.

"Ask for Pimms at the Bearded Lamb?" Stan stared. "And me like a father to you."

"You trying to get us killed, then?" Eustace asked mildly.

When they'd walked off into the sunshine, I hauled clean clothes out of my rucksack and struggled out of my wet ones. Byron wrinkled his nose and flung each article I passed him to dry onto the grass outside the pub. I finished up barefoot and contemplative. The two of us sat down on the second picnic table, the less rickety table out back of the pub. Byron handed me a can of soda water and cracked a cider for himself.

"Byron, I need to know. How exactly did you get Angelica away from me?"

"Oh, well, you know how it is. The tides of love flow back and forth."

"No, really. Did you romance her? Breathe in her ear? Say insulting things about my honour and stamina?"

"Never." Byron shot me a suspicious look. "We talked about

this. You gave me your promise never to attempt to get Angelica back again. Focus on Holly."

"Exactly. That's what I'm doing. And I promise not to violate your copyright with Angelica. Just tell me what you did to get her back."

Byron cleared his throat. He straightened his polo collar and managed somehow to look noble. "I simply asked her a question."

"This is important information. What question?"

"I don't want to tell you. It might hurt your feelings."

"You've never cared about my feelings before, and I don't see why you should begin now."

"Look, Spencer. There's nothing you or I can do to help with a decision as momentous as a woman deciding to leave her marriage. It's entirely up to her. She will have to make a difficult choice, maybe even an impossible one, and believe me she must do it on her own."

"But ... "

"If you try to help, you'll taint all possibility of future happiness. But you can ask a neutral question, in a supportive sort of way."

"As a friend?"

"As it were."

You mean to say you know of a question that I could ask her, which, once answered in a certain way, could result in future happiness?"

"You ask it, but she doesn't answer."

That sounded wrong to me, but I was still trying to pin down this amazing piece of knowledge that Byron, who never read a book, had somehow invented or discovered.

"And this might bring me a second chance at happiness?"

"It's not guaranteed."

"Byron, tell me."

He told me.

"But when shall I ask it?"

"You'll know the moment." He stood and set his empty cider bottle in the centre of the table and moved off, a long string bean in a polo shirt, hands in his pockets, heading to his car.

I called after him, "How long will I have to wait?"

Instead of an answer, I heard the sound of his car door and then his engine.

Byron was gone. I picked up my phone and read her email. I looked again at her picture. I reminded myself that Byron's was a story of success, when he won back the love of my ex-wife Angelica. He had been quite definite. He'd said I would have to wait.

But he had also said that I would know when the time was right.

I felt it might be. And if it was, I didn't want to miss this opportunity.

I typed a return message to Holly. "Still beautiful. Of course. But I remember you so well, as if it was yesterday, and in your picture you appear … " I paused, remembering the vision I'd had of the empty foundations of the Seven Swans. "… you appear to me to be on the verge of some kind of decision."

I typed the return bar.

And added, quoting Byron directly, "What are you going to do?"

Before I could add anything more, a hissing noise from behind caused me to turn sharply. I found myself much closer than I would like to be to an angry swan. Phone in hand, I untangled myself from the picnic bench and dashed barefoot towards the pub door, the swan in close pursuit. I had never before been attacked by a swan, and you'd think something with that many feathers would be harmless. But I'd rather be chased by an angry dog than ever again by a swan. It's something about the focus, the hiss, and the wingspan that makes you promise to heaven to be a better person if you escape the creature unharmed. I felt a jab like an icepick on my right thigh as I made it inside the pub entrance. Stan had done something to the door so that it closed now, and I thanked the man as I shut it behind me.

Now, to be a better man: do I send this question, *what are you going to do,* to Holly or not?

I wondered what the good equerry of the good Duke in 1758 would counsel me to do? But I recalled that his duty was not to advise, but simply to do what was best for his master.

Meanwhile, the swan flapped in fury outside the pub door, and I had a hard time concentrating. But one clear thought came to me: a person must be his own good equerry.

Before I could think anything else, I pressed *send.*

§

Spencer Stevens returns with a new mystery in time in Issue 20 of Pulp *Literature.*

FOR THE LOVE OF GREY

Anat Rabkin

Anat is a Vancouver-based artist and writer aspiring to tell stories that make you feel. As an immigrant to Canada, she finds she has often a different perspective on life than her North American counterparts. Movies, animation, books, comics, and tabletop roleplaying games all give her inspiration to tell new tales. The art of storytelling is taken for granted these days, its importance underplayed as mere entertainment. If she could put one thing on her business card that would rock her world, it'd be 'storyteller'. Two of her short comics have appeared in Pulp Literature: 'Forbidden Fruit' in Issue 9 and 'It Rained Then, Too' in Issue 13.

For the Love of Grey

She woke up too early. She always did. The painfully loud barks of a dog down the street started at the same time every morning... As soon as she was awake, the barking seemed less loud, as though this place was playing tricks on her.

This place.

The line was so long. It had taken days to get in. The government passing by with supplies. There was no sense in keeping supplies hoarded at this point.

Not at the end of the world.

She got up and stretched. Her bones ached. They always ached here.

Her room was barely larger than a van. A bed, a dresser, a writing desk. A grey cube to live out eternity in. She dressed in drab clothing that didn't really fit and certainly didn't flatter.

The bathroom at the end of the hall had a line. Of course it did. Instead she returned to her room, brushed her teeth with some water from her water bottle, and spat into a basin she had found the other day.

She could use the lavatory at work.

The way to work was dreary, as always. The grey sky only just brighter than the grey, square buildings. The streets were packed with tired people meandering their way to their employments. Were they also woken up by that same dog? The one that she couldn't find, since pets weren't allowed?

Or was that personal hell reserved for her?

She had spent a long time thinking about the way this place worked.

She did so today as well, while she waited for the bleary-eyed barista to give her a cup of unsatisfying, lukewarm coffee.

She thought about it as she transferred numbers from one sheet to another, double — and triple — checking her accuracy until she couldn't tell numbers from letters.

Then back to her square of grey.

She told herself she liked the grey. Over the next days she stopped on her way to and from work and studied the small, malnourished shrubs at the side of the road. She found beauty in their mangled, stunted leaves.

She found beauty in the weary faces at her side.

She wondered why the people around her chose this gate when the world ended. Why this gate and not the other? Did they feel they deserved this place?

Why would someone choose hell when heaven was an option?

When the Rapture came, they had all lined up for days. No fights, no war, not even panic. Like they had waited for this all their lives. People lined up as they chose. One gate to heaven, one to hell.

TV shows debated if there was actually any real choice. Perhaps people were compelled to choose one or the other.

But Lizzy knew why she'd chosen hell.

"There can't be heaven without a loss of humanity," she had argued with her best friend as they parted. "There can't ever be perfect joy without a goddamn lobotomy."

So she lined up for hell. Better to keep her own mind and be miserable than to lose herself and be drugged into merry oblivion.

She wondered how Beth was doing and hoped she was pleased with her choice. She had to be — wasn't that the definition of heaven? She no longer had the choice, perhaps, to be anything but happy.

It was that thought that triggered her love of grey.

She now set her alarm to wake up an hour early (an hour and fifteen minutes — thanks, dog) and spent that hour before work exploring the dull greyness.

Whatever this place was, she was discovering, it was imperfect. There were cracks in the streets, though never any cars. She stopped and studied the cracks. There were no roots that could have caused them, and no weather changes; it was always a dreary overcast day. What had caused the deformity? Was it a deliberate design? She found shapes in the cracks and made up stories.

She started smiling as she passed the largest crack.

In a sea of over-stressed, over-tired faces, she forced a smile and a greeting for the barista each morning. At first he didn't even acknowledge her, but now he was meeting her eye, his expression almost fearful. Expectant, perhaps.

She tried watering one of the stunted shrubs on the side of the path. She filled up her water bottle (which she had learned not to put in her purse, as it leaked only there), and gave it some water every day.

After a month of this, it was noticeably taller than its counterparts.

On her one day off a month, she met with a co-worker. She didn't particularly like this person, but Rosita was the only other person she had spoken to. She wondered sometimes if they were real, the people around her. Could they be constructs of this place, like the crack in the road? Were they there to keep her isolated? Or were they like her, lost in the endless grey of each day?

"I don't see why you try." Rosita frowned when Lizzy looked towards the outside patio of the mediocre restaurant. It was too cold to sit outside. Why have a patio, then? Was it part of someone's memory? Or was it there by design to make you long for something you couldn't have?

"Can you think of something better to do to pass an actual eternity?" was Lizzy's counter. Things were getting to her today.

The food was not great. A bit too sour for her taste. It was like an underripe lemon had been thoroughly squeezed over everything. The pop was on the verge of being too flat.

Perhaps to shove it in Rosita's face, she took her plate and stepped outdoors, gesturing that the other woman should follow. Rosita declined.

So Lizzy sat on the patio. It wasn't too cold, she told herself; it was just right. It was perfect. The cold ran into her bones, a brisk wind picking up. But it was invigorating. She felt it. It was better than feeling nothing at all. She leaned into her food and inhaled deeply. It didn't smell great. No, she decided. It smelled like the best food this restaurant had to offer. She took a spoonful and closed her eyes as she chewed. It tasted a little like the meat was bad, but she was determined to love it.

The next month, it was bitter. She had the same dish, and it was too bitter. It had started raining, too, so the patio was out. It was no longer too cold — now, it was humid. She decided she loved that, too.

It was another two months before she got the news. Her foreman, a large woman who had been struggling with her weight and ate a lunch of raw carrots each day, approached her. Lizzy wondered if she was a real person. Sometimes she wondered if she herself was real anymore.

"I have to let you go," the foreman said nervously.

Lizzy was shocked. Work was assigned by living blocks, and there was no option to quit. They were provided with no food, other than work lunches, and paid just enough money that they slowly went into debt. There were modest luxuries, like the morning coffee and sometimes a restaurant for everyone's different day off per month, but the money they earned never seemed to be enough.

"How will I eat?" she inquired. "Do I continue to live here?"

"I don't know," said her foreman. "I just got a letter. Please leave." She turned and all but ran away.

Lizzy returned to her cube to find her belongings outside. Her key did not unlock the door. She picked up her suitcase, the same one she had packed to stand in line for the Rapture, and wheeled it away.

There was a park down the street, with mostly dead plants and a bench that was just narrow enough to cut off circulation to her legs.

Was this the price of trying to enjoy hell?

How would she eat? An eternity of starvation without death seemed awful. No, she couldn't convince herself she liked that.

She sat on the awful bench and thought. That night, she slept on the bench. The bench was hard and the night was cold. She was miserable.

The next morning, she went looking for the dog.

She left her suitcase under the bench at the park. If someone wanted it, they were welcome to it. She was beginning to get angry at this place. It was acting like a petulant child.

She spent the entire day exploring each block around the living block. Empty residential buildings lined the outlying areas. All of them seem to have been deserted for a long time, their windows boarded up. She wondered if anyone had ever lived in them, or if they were there to remind them of long-lost homes.

When the houses ended, the road continuing into grey, featureless hills, she found the damn dog.

It was three dogs, lounging in a yard. The last house on the street. They were all mongrels, with large jowls and vicious little eyes. They were perhaps siblings, as they looked nearly identical. The yard was fenced, and though the house looked long-neglected, the dogs had collars and seemed well fed. Their fur shone with health. When they saw her, all three went berserk, running at the fence and barking, snarling, saliva thrown out of their teeth-filled mouths.

She managed to stay only a few moments before she fled.

She gathered her suitcase from beneath the bench and went back to the residences, asking people as they returned from work if she could stay with them. Most ignored her, others turned away.

She slept on the doorstep of the building, and it was cold.

The next day she changed her mind. Hell would not win.

She left her suitcase on the doorstep of the residences.

She went to the outskirts of town and found the yard with the dogs. They lost it again when they saw her, barking and growling furiously. She sat outside the fence, and waited.

After a few hours, she left them barking still.

Lizzy found a house, a few down from the dogs. It was one she liked, with a fence and a little yard. Climbing the fence to unlock the gate was easy, though she scraped her knee painfully. Of course she did.

She was hungry.

She picked up a metal pipe in the yard. After a lot of swearing and effort, she managed to break the boards on a window.

She feared the inside would be too dilapidated, with holes in the roof and water damage, but she squashed the feeling down. Even if that was the case, there were others. Perhaps this place would be nice inside.

Before her eyes, the interior of the house flickered. As the boards fell, nothing but grey met her eyes, like an error in reality. For a moment it showed her the interior just as she feared: broken floors and light streaming through holes in the ceiling. Then it flickered again, seeming to settle on a dusty old home with furniture covered in a layer of decay. It smelled of dust and mould. For a moment, the dogs a few homes down were silent.

Lizzy climbed into the house and surveyed it. It reminded her of her grandmother's house. She had hated going there as a child. Her grandmother had wanted her father to sire sons, and Lizzy was never enough.

Lizzy kicked the threadbare sofa. It hurt her toe through her Mary Jane work shoes.

She unlocked the door and set about cleaning the place. She decided she loved it.

The house fought her, tooth and nail.

The floors creaked, the ceiling leaked. The bed, though tidy, smelled of strange things. The kitchen had dishes, but corroded, unnameable residue was forever stuck on them.

"You're going to have to do better than that," she said, rolling up her sleeves and setting to wash them.

She was surprised when the taps worked, though not surprised that the water ran only cold.

She dusted, she mopped, she moved things around. When she was done, it was about time to return for her suitcase. Everyone was returning from work at that time, and she watched them file into the building.

Rosita found her and gave her a plastic plate covered with another plastic plate. There was a whole serving of food in there. Rosita had tears in her eyes. Before Lizzy could speak, Rosita ran off.

She gathered her suitcase and, carrying the plate in her other hand, returned to her commandeered home.

She tripped on the way. Of course she did. The food fell to the ground. She picked it up and ate it at her dining table at home anyway. What, was she going to catch hell germs?

The next day she dug up her shrub from the side of the road. She was the one who watered it, so it was her shrub. She planted it in her garden. She weeded it, so it was her garden. The dogs, perhaps smelling her, barked incessantly.

She went and sat with them for a few more hours. They were

calmer the next day, their barks settling down to growls after some minutes.

The next day she pushed her way in with the work crowd and went directly to the kitchens. The food was already ready, though no one was preparing it.

She helped herself, grabbing some extra for later, and left. She feared being chased out if discovered.

She loved this place.

All the books left behind on her shelf were poorly written by people she had never heard of. When she found herself enjoying one, the next chapter would be missing critical pages, usually around the interesting bits. She couldn't help but laugh.

Days went by. Hell was losing its steam.

The dogs now seemed used to her presence, greeting her with a half-hearted bark or growl then sitting by the fence. She even reached over one day to try and scratch one of their ears (she couldn't tell them apart), but he snapped at her.

Her home was always dirty, the floors uneven. The ever-present grime on the dishes, stubbornly sticky no matter how much she scrubbed, made her queasy. But she was determined to love it.

Her shrub was growing quickly and recovering a bit of colour, she liked to think. Food was plentiful if she didn't mind being yelled at or shoved when seen. Sometimes it was one of her previous co-workers, yelling at her for stealing though there was never a shortage. She had an endless supply of chilled tap water, though she knew the tap was trying extra hard to make it taste more tappy. She had conversations with the tap.

The house had no electricity, so when it got dark she had to stumble her way through. Her toes found things to hit even when she knew the corridor was empty. She started shuffling slowly instead, pushing her toes ahead.

Hell countered with a splinter from the old wooden floors. She responded by making slippers out of her old coat.

Hell made it colder at night. She broke into five more houses until she convinced herself the last thing she wanted to find was a pile of rank, mouldering blankets. When they appeared in the next house, she took them home and washed them. Afterwards they were perfect.

One of the dogs had let her pet it the other day, and her love of grey was getting so pronounced that she could swear she saw a piece of blue sky the day before.

She had no money, but she spent some mornings at the coffee shop, sipping a forgotten cup (someone always forgot their cup) and watching the people mill by. She smiled at them, greeted the barista, watched them. It was never her preferred order of coffee, even though there were only a few choices. It was always too dark, or too sweet, or too watered down, but she decided she loved all of them.

When she returned to her home that day, a single ray of sun shone down on her small garden. She squealed and clapped, dancing around.

A few houses over, perhaps startled by the sound, the dogs gave a couple of barks.

She loved this.

THE THEFT OF CONFIDENCE

Soramimi Hanarejima

Soramimi Hanarejima *is a writer of innovative fiction and the author of* Visits to the Confabulatorium, *a fanciful story collection from Montag Press Collective. Soramimi's recent work has appeared in various literary magazines, including* Panoply, Foliate Oak, *and* Rigorous.

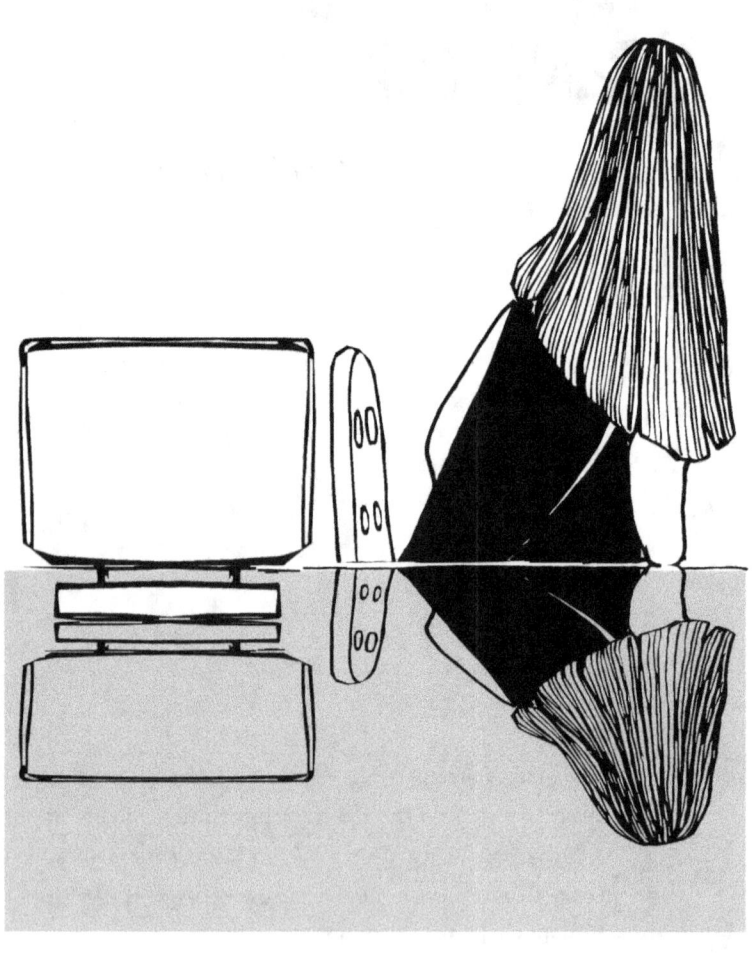

ᖛHE THEFT OF CONFIDENCE

Now that the loss of her confidence follows a clear pattern, you need to figure out how that pattern can be broken. That means figuring out the rest of the pattern, the middle of it. You know the beginning and the end of the daily cycle all too well now.

She starts the day full of confidence, just brimming with it during your breakfast dates together. She wields such fantastic amounts of self-assurance over blueberry pancakes and granola with yogurt, like she's ready to negotiate multiple high-stakes deals simultaneously. She speaks with bright eyes and fluency in an impassioned dialect of authority that intersperses gestures decisively among forthright words. You love it. So much that, as someone who often needs semi-regular confidence boosts, you could get jealous.

But you don't. Instead, you get concerned. Because after work, when you meet no longer for cocktails but for the coffee she badly needs, she's got precious little confidence left. Barely enough to improvise a great dinner with the miscellaneous ingredients on hand in her kitchen. Doubt suggests that the two of you dine out instead.

This can't continue. Those morning displays of confidence suit her so well. You can't bear to see her regress to her previous self: the obsessive worrier always accompanied by an entourage of insecurities. For now, sleep replenishes her confidence, but who knows how restorative slumber will be in the long term?

You need to determine what happens to her confidence during business hours.

So off you go, sleuthing about her workplace, incognito as the ubiquitous office intern. You've lured away the actual intern with a week-long career strategy consultation conducted by the private coach you hired, which buys you a good amount of time for your detective work — time that ends up being necessary. It takes you a good several days to even begin making progress.

The lengthiness of your investigation is due to two factors: you start off looking in the wrong places, and the loss of confidence happens more subtly than you expected. You thought it would be some challenging project or demanding client relationship that her confidence is poured into then lost to a lack of progress or absence of feedback. But after hours of attentively attending meetings, peeking frequently into her office, and tagging along on her errands, you see nothing of the sort. Exhausted by all the close yet fruitless observation, you space out during coffee-break chit-chat and eat lunch with delirious delight, needing the calories and relishing the thick umami of cafeteria lasagne.

Whole days go by without any leads. You see her confidence going into only high-quality work and thoughtful conversations.

Then a mid-morning encounter in the office kitchen catches your attention.

She's in the midst of preparing a little snack when a co-worker strolls in.

"Well, if it isn't the darling of the division," he says. "You ought to treat us to a seminar on just how you stay *such* a paragon of productivity here! Be sure to mention these stroopwafel breaks, for *surely* they are the secret to keeping your performance formidable — that's French for wonderful."

He pours himself a cup of coffee and leaves.

Was that a compliment to her conscientiousness or a swipe at subpar progress? Or simply melodramatic jest?

For a moment, she seems just as puzzled as you.

Then she returns her attention to the task at hand: breaking up the stroopwafel she's holding into pieces that can handily be eaten with sliced strawberries using a spoon.

It takes you a few more incidents with this co-worker to determine that the incident in the kitchen is typical of his interactions with her. And indeed, his behaviour is deliberately equivocal — and ultimately malicious. He wields a jocularity that's ambiguous, interpretable as idiosyncratic or passive aggressive in the service of furtively elevating his confidence. A remark about her conduct here, a suggestion on project priorities there, a joke about her reputation now and then. Are they awkward or arrogant? Snippy or sincere? Hard to say, so she gives him the benefit of the doubt and responds with geniality and confidence. But his discomfiting tone insinuates disparagement and exacts its toll, lowering her confidence relative to his, allowing him to sap her of it.

The pattern then comes into complete clarity. He's siphoning away her confidence, discreetly drawing it off with insecurity, creating the necessary confidence differential under the guises of constructive criticism and banter during coffee breaks, coincidental encounters in the hallway, and lunchtime.

You should have known. You usually recognize the type.

He's the kind of person who thinks that confidence is zero-sum, that it can only be gained at another's expense. So he fancies himself a sort of sly embezzler depleting her account of personal certainty by prodding her to make semi-frequent withdrawals that he can surreptitiously snatch away to build up his cache of confidence.

Your first impulse is to give her your shell of indifference to deploy in his presence. But you want a solution that's less cumbersome, more automatic, and more deterring—even detrimental, if possible. A few hours later, it hits you while you're drinking a cup of revitalizing coffee. *Coffee.* When you have coffee with her this evening, you'll spike hers with moxie. You have plenty left in your cache, and you can easily make a trip home to get some before you meet her at the usual café.

You can see it now. You walk over to the counter to pick up the beverages the barista has just finished brewing. There you lace her mug with a generous splash from the flask full of moxie that's been hiding in your jacket pocket. Then you bring both mugs to the café table where she's waiting, tired and eager for delicious, soothing coffee.

This stuff is bound to give her confidence more of an edge, turning it jagged with sarcasm in the face of anything threatening to lower it.

The only problem is that she might get attitudey with other co-workers, and you're not sure if it will be taken as charisma or defiance. Will she be seen as exhibiting character or impertinence? She can probably get away with some sass for a little while. From what you've seen of her workdays, her diligence and agreeability must have earned her enough social capital redeemable in the form of idiosyncrasy credits.

But what if her work relationships can't take that strain? you wonder.

The answer comes almost immediately, and you smile at the arrival and appeal of what will be your backup plan.

The moxie can be put to use another way — into settling this matter the way your fifteen-year-old self would: with pranks. A few swigs from your stash, and you'll be ready to hijinks the guy into thinking he's jinxed. A 'misplaced' report draft here, a copier 'accident' there, a 'misdialled' phone call to him now and then. Maybe a computer virus or task chair 'malfunction' or sudden spam deluge. There are plenty of options. And all that will just be the beginning. The prelude to giving his confidence a good rattle, unsteadying it enough that he can no longer rob her of confidence.

Your smile widens. You're tempted to make this your primary plan.

After a moment of reverie, however, the mischievous glee relinquishes its hold upon your thoughts, and they return to your first plan. As much as you want to have some adolescent fun, she could do with some diversification in her portfolio of reputation capital here. You're sure that if you can get the dosing of moxie right, the original plan promises good fun for her.

EMBERS

Misha Handman

Misha Handman has been writing fantasy and mystery stories for as long as he can remember. When not writing, he works as a manager for the performing arts in Victoria, BC, helping other artists bring their own works to their audiences.

$\mathcal{E}$MBERS

A woman sat by the fire, as the night closed in around her.

It was a small fire. A few blocks of wood piled around the now-burned kindling, surrounded by grey stones. The woman sat on a log, poking at the fire with a long, slender spear forged of white metal and silver. She was older than she had been at her first vigil. Her hair was greyer, and she felt the cold in her joints. She had changed. But the night was the same.

She watched as the darkness swallowed the stars above and tendrils of shadow surrounded her camp. Embers drifted from the fire, and as they passed beyond the ring of light they winked out.

"Hello again," she said.

"Hello again," the darkness responded. Its voice was the same as always: smooth as silk, with the pressure of a whisper and a hint of music to it. "Shall we dance?"

"Not yet." The woman gestured to the flames. "The fires are not gone."

"They are low, keeper. You have built them poorly."

"When the fires are high, you don't approach."

The night chuckled. "Not until I have eaten my fill," it agreed. "But I understand. I have watched you through our fights, keeper. You are not the fighter that you once were. You are old. There is no shame in fearing me."

"No fear," the woman said. She pulled her spear out of the flames, looking at its red-hot blade. The shadows pulled back a half-step as she turned it and then replaced it in the heart of the campfire. "I'm just deciding whether to fight you tonight."

A chuckle from the shadows. "Of course you will fight. And this time, you will die."

"Everyone does, eventually."

"I will devour you. I will swallow the light that flickers in your chest."

"You may," the woman agreed. "And then you will be alone."

"Then I will leave, and seek out the people below, and take their light, and onwards until the sun itself does not rise."

"And then?"

For the first time, she felt the shadows falter.

"And then ... I will have won."

"And you will still be alone."

"And so shall you," the darkness hissed.

"No," the woman said. "I will be gone, to whatever place lies beyond this world."

"Then I will chase you there!" the shadows snarled.

"Why? I'm already here."

"What?"

"If you want to see me, you don't have to do all of that. I'm already here."

"But you won't be."

"Not if you drink my light, no."

"No."

The fire began to gutter. The woman pulled her spear out again and stuck it in the dirt.

"You are a fool."

"Trust has to begin somewhere."

Silence settled over the clearing. Beyond the fading ring of light there was nothing but a deep, endless void. The woman watched, and waited.

"Put another log on the fire," the shadows said. "And then we will discuss this new madness of yours."

The woman smiled. She stood with a faint groan and walked to the logs stacked beside the fire. Taking one, she added it to the campfire and watched the fire slowly grow again. "It will be a long night," she said.

"The longest," the shadows agreed. "But then, it will be a long discussion."

"The first of many," the woman said.

ONE SAFE PLACE

Erin Slaughter

Erin Slaughter *holds an MFA in Creative Writing from West-*
ern Kentucky University. She has been a finalist for Glimmer
Train's *Very Short Fiction Contest and was nominated for a*
Best of the Net Award and a Pushcart Prize. You can find her
writing in River Teeth, Bellingham Review, Sundog
Lit, Tishman Review, *and elsewhere. She is the author of*
two poetry chapbooks: Elegy for the Body *(Slash Pine Press,*
2017) and the forthcoming GIRLFIRE *(dancing girl press,*
2018), and is editor and co-founder of the literary journal The
Hunger. *She lives and teaches writing in Nashville.*

One Safe Place

My foot is grinding into the pedal of Max's battered Chevy, the intestines of the old car sputtering and gurgling under the pressure. Max is sitting next to me in the front seat, clutching at his arm and bleeding into the black upholstery. He's mostly quiet, except for little gasps and grits of his teeth when we hit a bump in the road. There is only Max, his dark hair damp with sweat, curling in the delicate places behind his ears and sticking to his forehead. Then there is the endless road, stretching out like a tightrope through the desert as we hurtle ourselves across it under the bleached dawn sky.

"Talk to me," I say. "You're being too quiet."

"Drive faster," he says.

"Working on it. This piece-of-shit car—"

"Hey," he says. "Don't talk shit about my car."

Even knuckle-deep in his own blood, Max would defend this iron death-trap. The air conditioner has been broken since 1985, the speedometer since four Thanksgivings ago. Right now it's chugging out its last breath, hopefully far and fast enough to save Max's. I don't know why he thought any of us would survive to reach the coast.

An hour ago.

Just outside of Paradise, Nevada, we were twenty-three hundred miles and five days gone, and we were running out of money. I knew this, even though Max insisted it wasn't true. The brick of cash we left New Jersey with was now a single roll of ten-dollar bills nestled into the breast pocket of Max's flannel shirt and quickly depleting. He carelessly circled the bills around his pointer finger until they stuck like that. It was all in pursuit of the promised land, Santa Monica.

"This is for getting there," he said. "The important thing is getting there."

Scattered along the lonely highway were abandoned houses, their wooden bones split open, the kinds of places only nature fights to inhabit. We saw them in each town we drove through. My fingers trailed over the peeling floral wallpaper in the two-storey farmhouse, whose blown-open window frame we had easily climbed through. Painted violets speckled the walls like bruises.

Old records, some still in their sleeves, littered the wooden floorboards. The kitchen floor had sunken in, sucking an orange sofa down with it. Max tested the stairs with one foot, but his boot crashed through the first rotten step.

"Well," he said, smiling, "I guess we'll never know what's lurking around up there."

I opened my mouth to reply but it was swallowed in fragmented noise from outside: a man's distant holler and then the yell of his rifle cracking open the night sky. Max's eyes went wide as they met mine, frozen in a single panicked moment. We bolted through the sunken kitchen and out the back door, leaping across the overgrown yard to the car. The rifle blasted again and I saw Max fall in the grass, reaching for the car handle. For one sharp instant, I was sure he was dead, and then he stumbled up, making tiny, strangled noises, slid his body into the front seat, and we sped off through the grass. It wasn't until our wheels found pavement again that I saw the blood pooling on his shirt.

"Hey," I say. "Stay with me."

He says, "Damn it. Goddamn it, Andrew."

"That's good," I say. "You've got to stay conscious."

"Find a place to pull over. Drive off the road. Fuck—just make something happen." He winces and bites down on his lower lip. More blood.

"We're going to the hospital."

"No! No, I can't, I told you. I won't go back to Tabernacle—"

I don't blame him. The town we grew up in is a wasteland of historic buildings and empty streets dropped into the New Jersey Pine Barrens. And he had been stuck there a lot longer than I had, I remembered.

"Dude, you're bleeding. A lot."

"Well, maybe there's some things I didn't tell you, okay? People who would be looking for me, would take me back. I'm sorry, but we can't. We can't go to the hospital." He stares out the window, purposefully avoiding my gaze.

"Max . . . " I begin, but he looks at me and says, "Please, just—just give me this. We'll figure it out. Just get us someplace safe."

"Okay, I get it. It's okay. Hold on," I say. The wheels pound relentlessly against the asphalt, a kind of lullaby. "What does it feel like?"

"Like a hot, white cut," he says. "Like a goddamn supernova is gushing from my body, and the light won't stop pouring out."

Yesterday.

He wanted to run so we ran, and he wanted to see the Grand Canyon so we drove through the night from Amarillo, through the neon rest stops, the quiet restaurants, the overpasses like brick after concrete brick on the skyline. Max slept, the side of his face smashed against the cool glass, his hand coiled around the seatbelt the same way an infant holds its mother's finger.

Just before sunrise, Max sat up, and it was all there in front of us. Pale dawn light hung fragile around our bodies as we walked towards the edge.

He's mostly cynical and callous, but every so often he fills with a childish wonder, and the crinkles in the corners of his eyes fade like rivers erased from a map. In one breathtaking motion, Max's smile bloomed over the crevasse.

Golden sunlight broke and spilled over those red-painted ridges, the peaks huddled close like tiny villages and the molten river slicing through at the impossible bottom of it all. I looked down, feeling swallowed. Max began to cry. I didn't look up.

"You want to know my best memory, growing up?" His voice cut up, his breathing jagged.

"What?"

"When my dad was in jail the first time for selling those fake bonds—you remember?"

"Yeah, I remember," I said.

"Well, my mom took me to Florida, to the beach. And it was kind of a shitty beach, but I was, like, seven, right? My mom made a big deal out of it, too. She rented this RV and we camped out right across from it … The sand was right there when we stepped out of the RV, I remember that. So anyway, we were there, and my mom started flirting with this muscle dude, and he came over and hung out with us for a while. He was, like, super nice to me and helped me build this huge, amazing sandcastle. It was the best day of my life. I didn't know he was trying to fuck my mom, didn't even notice when they left me and went off to the RV later, because I was so excited just to be there." He wiped his face against the back of his shirt sleeve. "What kind of shitty childhood is that? That's my best memory. Was my best."

He inhaled as if trying to breathe in the canyon dust, to hold it all inside his lungs.

"Just … thanks. Thanks for doing this," he said. "It's amazing, isn't it?"

"Yeah," I said. "It's really something."

It was beautiful, I guess, but it felt more like the absence of something. Max's eyes were bright with whatever it was people came here to find, but feeling things so eloquently, so intensely, seemed like some grand secret I wasn't privy to. Something I was no longer in touch with.

A dollop of green neon breaks the landscape up ahead: a Days Inn.

"This is the place," I tell him.

He mumbles in reply.

I leave Max in the car, check in, and pay with cash. The room costs $80, almost everything we have left, and as I hand the money to the receptionist I get an uneasy feeling that I choke down, remembering it's our only option. Remembering Max's face when he begged me to do this with him alone.

I pull around to the back of the building and pop the trunk, the plastic room key clamped between my teeth, and sling my duffel bag and Max's over one shoulder. I slip the half-empty bottle of Jack Daniels into the zipper pocket of my bag. Max looks like a rag doll hunching over the dashboard, and for a second I choke on something, something like dread or longing. I swallow it. Is it possible he has gotten paler in the last ten minutes? All his blood seems to have drained into the fabric of his green flannel shirt.

"Come on," I say, helping him from the car with my free arm. "Come on, it's all right, I got you."

It's a long trek through the scorched parking lot up the metal staircase to the motel room. I can imagine myself as Atlas, all that is left of the world draped over my shoulders and seeming heavier with every step, the tacky yellow paint from the metal railings chipping off underneath my fingers.

Three days ago.

We blazed across the midlands, burning through every decaying town in our path, sweeping through cities made of glass, those bright sparkling headache lights clustered behind us in the distance. The dark blue Chevy roared like a rapturous beast, devouring miles in fistfuls. We cranked the windows down by hand, blared 'Tomorrow Never Knows' so loudly that fifteen miles away they could feel it pumping through their veins. Half the country passed in a blur of melting sunlight and diamond stars embedded all over the American sky.

We were escaping a place, but it was really an escape from our skin, from the dark tunnels of lives that would have us live and die standing still. Now, as asphalt stretched over Kansas, I was seeing all of that crumble. I was seeing the dusty red future flatten itself out in front of me like a canvas. I was singing The Beatles as Rome burned in the rearview.

What I remember most was Max, knuckles white on the steering wheel, hair in a flurry, dark brown eyes lit ablaze. Screaming out to the song at the top of my lungs, what I remember thinking is this: I hope we fucking crash, I hope we die, I hope it's messy and unavoidable, our flesh and bones and limbs mangled together for all eternity. Because as long as I live and breathe, nothing will ever be better than this. Nothing will ever again feel like that last mile — wild-eyed, reckless. Free.

Twin lamps on twin night stands on each side of the sunken bed, white coffee-maker on the bathroom counter, white Styrofoam cups wrapped in plastic on the wooden desk; if you folded the hotel room in half, each side would mirror the other. Max slumps off my shoulder onto the king-sized mattress. A trail of wet blood flecks the linoleum entry. Max is spread out on the generic hotel bedspread — brown with jade slivers, like leaves at the bottom of a lake. His shirt is ruined. I bend down to take it off him, my fingers intentional, trying hard to be whispers on his skin. He winces anyway.

The wound is a crater the size of a quarter in the flesh of his upper arm. I've seen things like this in movies, worse even, but here and now it's terrifying. I cross the room, come back to the bedside with a wooden chair and my duffel bag.

"Here," I say, placing the bottle of whiskey in his good hand. "Drink up."

He doesn't question it, takes a gulp. The amber liquid sloshes around the glass bottle. Another gulp.

"How're we gonna do this?" he asks.

I take the pocket knife from my bag and begin ripping Max's ruined shirt into strips. His watery eyes shine in the yellow lamplight, waiting for an answer.

One week ago.

Max met me at my apartment door, his laughter hollow, his hair too short. His jaw all angles and edges. He walked in like it hadn't been almost three years, and in that instant, it didn't feel like it had been. There was a warmth about him, the smell of his childhood bedroom preserved in his voice's soft sarcasm. He asked me how my day had been. We ate white rice from plastic bowls.

Then he offered me a new life like he was offering me a soda, and when a boy like that asks you to run away with him, you do. You leave your cell phone on the kitchen counter and throw your clothes into a bag without bothering to fold them. He asked me to run, so I ran, and I didn't ask where we were going, or why, because it didn't matter. I was going with him.

I want to stop apologizing. I pour the warm whiskey over Max's wound and he yelps like a hurt puppy and I say sorry. I dip the tip of the knife into the angry red hole in his arm and he jerks it away, and I have to cuff his wrist to the bed with my free hand

and watch as he writhes like an animal trying to escape from its skin, all the while saying *sorry, I'm sorry, I'm so sorry*, muttering it like a prayer until my lips are chapped.

Thankfully the wound isn't that deep, but the flesh around it puckers, clinging to the bullet. I try to keep my hands from shaking, hoping Max doesn't notice. My eyes flicker to him, but his own are pressed tightly shut. The blood covering my hands smells like sour fruit, sticky and hot.

I can't help but think of going hunting with my grandfather. I must have been thirteen or fourteen. I couldn't shoot the deer, not when it had seen us, so he did it for me. A veteran, both of war and hunting, neither the shot nor the carnage startled him. He cut the belly of the buck open and the insides flooded out, then in the same breath he began methodically separating the flesh from the bone, piece by piece. I stood and watched as he worked, amazed and fearful at how the animal became less of an animal with each flick of his knife. Knowing that we all look this way on the inside, inanimate bone and meat.

The blood keeps coming and I keep wiping it away, trying to find the source, the bullet nestled somewhere inside. I keep digging and keep offering Max whiskey, his free hand trembling as he struggles to tip the bottle to his mouth. Can anything keep him warm when he shivers that way? He is making noises that I promise not to remember. The bullet is still buried in his arm, and we are drowned in the yellow lamplight, the dislocated feeling that a whole summer has passed through the dirty orange curtains of the hotel room.

"Andrew, I want to tell you what happened in Tabernacle," he says. "Don't."

"Don't you want to know why —?"

"No," I say.

"Why not?"

"Because it doesn't matter."

The whiskey baptizes the wound and the blood keeps coming. I am still digging, still carving him open, still searching for what's hidden there, shirking from the light.

Last year.

I took a job at a customer service call centre, and the only thing I remember about those six months of dial tones and sanitized headsets was the map of North America on my gray cubicle wall. While I typed notes into the computer and sent out free coupons to angry customers, I traced the highways from coast to coast with my gaze, formulating some kind of personal manifest destiny. I opened a savings account. I was good at my job. I thought a lot about faking my death.

I came home each evening and climbed the four sets of stairs to my apartment. I lay in bed and listened to the train howl in the distance. Darkness and sunlight came on a loop, without reason. It all comes back in images like this, days recycled and melded into weeks, everything eating everything.

One day, I was getting into my car to go to the grocery store, and I realized it was Max's birthday. I had forgotten. I stared at my phone for a while, not sure what to say. I knew the way it would play out, as it always did: I would overcome my pounding pulse to text him, and wait all day, all week, for him not to text back. I put my phone away, and I was proud of myself, proud for having forgotten his birthday to begin with. It was raining, and I sat in my car, watching the sky's blues and oranges melt across the windshield.

I wondered what Max was doing.

I wipe the sweat from my forehead with the back of my arm. Max is clammy, but he's still cursing and occasionally fisting the sheets. His moans are growing softer, more desperate. He's tired. We both are.

My hands are all over his skin, raw, hot in the lamplight. I can't get the bullet out, I think, for what truly feels like weeks. I can't, and then I do. With a pocket knife and a pair of tweezers, I finally purge the black pearl of lead. It's so small I nearly want to laugh.

"I want to see it," Max says.

I hold it in the palm of my hand, up to the light. Max smiles weakly with one corner of his mouth, and his eyes go hazy, and he falls backwards on the bed.

Three years ago.
I want to tell you this story without having to be in it.

I don't want it to be about me, so let's say it's about you. Let's say you are at the party, the radio cooing some soft melody in the starlit back yard. Sweet poisonous whiskey calms your muscles, while laughter and the smell of barbecue rise in waves through the night air. In the corner of your eye, the golden blur of fairy lights pinned to the fence, a couple swaying barefoot in the grass.

You go inside the house to grab a beer from the fridge. Max

invited you here, but you haven't seen him all night. In fact, you haven't seen him in almost a year.

Your hand closes around the neck of the bottle, the glass eerie green in the refrigerator light. Every surface of the house is white, and reminds you of a morgue.

You're already drunk, too drunk, when you see Max in the dark hallway. Your legs like stilts, your mouth numb. You hug him and feel his stubble scratch your own freshly-shaven cheek. His body is so soft, feels like home wrapped around yours. You press your mouth against his, and you don't even know what you are doing, can't feel anything but you just *want* and he pushes you away from him and you stumble, hear the back of your head thud against the wall. You have ruined everything. You know this.

You can't breathe, so you run out into the road. The chilly air stings. You lie down in the gravel, smelling gasoline, the sky spinning. There are no cars.

He doesn't follow you.

"I owe you," Max says. He's bandaged, strips of his shirt wrapped around his swollen arm tight enough to stop the bleeding for now. He's lying on the bed in navy boxers, sipping sink water from a Styrofoam cup.

"It's fine," I say. "It's nothing, don't worry about it."

"I mean, I literally owe you my life after that," he says. There is a part of me I hate, a part of me that feels like I've won something when he says it.

"We'll call it even," I say, trying to smile. Max's ribs make shadows on his skin in the dim fluorescent light, and he's trying to smile. He's so pale, almost seems made of moonlight.

I don't say, *I don't expect anything.* I don't say, *You know what I want and that I'll never say it.*

I say, "I'm going to take a shower."

Years and years and years.
Max's hands ruffling his hair in the mirror. *Elegantly dishevelled*, he called it, like he had named a planet, cured hunger. The buttons that stuck on the TV remote and Max's fingers: angry, tireless, gentle without trying. Playing tag in the yard, our socks damp and our knees grass-stained. Max at thirteen handing me a cigarette in the woods, nicked from his dad's stash in the garage, holding it up to his lips as if he knew how. Max's feet rustling under the blankets on the couch as he tried to fall asleep. *It's a comfort thing*, he said. Max's fingernails, elegant and dirt-embedded after his dad, as a punishment, made him spend four hours digging a hole in the backyard big enough for him to stand in. We were ten. We were twenty-one when he showed up to my mom's funeral holding the hand of a blonde girl named Shelby. They sat in the back pew, whispering almost-laughter, and left before the service was over.

When I get out of the shower, Max is asleep on top of the covers with the TV on, the room bathed in flickering shades of blue. An old cartoon plays on the screen, and with the sound turned off the characters scramble around, looking frightened.

Still wet, I lie down next to him. I can feel the warmth coming off his skin where my face rests next to his uninjured arm. He smells of sweat, of wildness. A bruise the size of a fingerprint purples underneath his collarbone.

He's sort of innocent like this, the way twenty-six years of pain and chaos slide off his face in sleep. You wouldn't know he was beautiful unless you saw him up close this way, unguarded. His long eyelashes, nose with the slightest crook to it, wet red lips looking stained and savage. His torso is all sliding muscle tectonic plates, all plains and peaks and plateaus. He has always seemed this way to me, even at seven years old and seventeen. He is blinding.

I brush a floppy strand of hair out of his face. His eyelash flutters against his cheek.

People are just people. You can't just open them up and create a safe place from the world. People are greedy and hungry and selfish, and they don't see the things that are right in front of them until it's too late, until the moment has passed and the silence tastes like the sharp twang of metal in your mouth. But there should be a way to feel grace under someone else's skin, to discard your own to be closer to their bones. There should be one safe place in the world, and it should be inside of love, but it isn't. So what do we do now? Where do we begin?

YOU DON'T KNOW
YOUR LIFE ANYWAY

Kelli Allen

Kelli Allen's *work has appeared in numerous journals in the US and internationally. She is Poetry Editor for* The Lindenwood Review *and directs River Styx's Hungry Young Poets series. Her chapbook,* Some Animals, *won the 2016 Etchings Press Prize. Her chapbook,* How We Disappear, *won the 2016 Damfino Press chapbook award. Her full-length poetry collection,* Otherwise, Soft White Ash, *arrived from John Gosslee Books in 2012 and was nominated for the Pulitzer Prize. Her latest book is* Imagine Not Drowning *(C&R Press, 2017). You can find her at kelli-allen.com.*

'You don't know your life anyway' is a response poem to Nicholas Christian's 'Wassail in Ink', which appeared in Issue 15 of Pulp Literature. *Kelli and Nick frequently travel the globe looking for an encouraging adventure.*

You don't know your life anyway

It was early and the extension of you was less,
and wet, twitch thumping between my cheek
and your thigh. We'll go alone hunting spring elk.

We share certain heroes in the wild way epics
are memorized in classroom caves far south
of here. Curtains above my bed are a misunderstanding.

Pelicans reach far back into the throat, too. Knocking
light against oak means more than knuckles finding
copper pots, steel blades hinting at rust, at long nights.

TATTOO

John Davies

John Davies was born in Birkenhead, UK, and has had work published in Crannóg, The Manchester Review, Rosebud, Orbis, The Pedestal, QU Literary Magazine, Apex, and Grain. In 2016 he was runner-up in the Cheshire Prize for Literature, and he won the RTÉ Guide / Penguin Ireland Short Story Competition. He organises a regular creative writing group in Navan, Ireland, which can be found on Twitter: @Bulls_Arse.

TATTOO

Nothing as obvious as the letting of blood
for these brothers by way of initiation,
wrists crossed as the warm wetness seeped
into Swiss Army Knife rust.
Instead, a ragged blue circle stabbed
into the back of each boy's hand,
held steady to deter any act of cowardice.
Doubtful the ten-year-old tattooist
had reached the top of his trade;
needle made white-hot in the corporation yard
bonfire, pot of ink pocketed from class.
Whichever one of them stepped up first
to prove this wasn't a game,
stomaching agony as the needle
snaketoothed into skin, the soft gristle,
ink floundering in the bloodstream;
took this solemn ceremony as the end
of time passing. In simple design, the blue spot
the start of a new understanding.

Forty-five years on, we have brought you back
to the Birkenhead street names of your stories.
Passing the corporation yard's spilt blood and ink,
the ritual site buried beneath new homes;
gone voices rising through the floorboards.
In this makeshift chapel,
as if to show off the tattoo
they have placed your hands
one over the other,
which I now smother in my own and rub
that they should not be so cold.
Rub the spot as you must have done
when a new wound,
determined not to cry.
It's not so bad after a while, you said
to the others still waiting in line;
already tending the backs of their hands,
where the blue spot would begin to travel
as the flesh grew.

LINEMAN

Susan Pieters

Sue is a founding editor of Pulp Literature. She wrote this short piece as a tribute to Bob Thurber, who has faithfully volunteered to serve as judge for Pulp Literature's Hummingbird Flash Fiction Prize for the last three years. The happy results of that contest are printed later in this issue.

$\mathcal{L}$INEMAN

I stayed on the ground, while Bob looped his binding around the pole like a lumberjack, climbing three steps before he swung his rope up. The steel in his boots pierced the wooden pole like he was Wolverine, but he shifted from side to side, outmatched in a dance with a giant.

People started to gather around. It was like watching a spider climb glass.

He topped out and felt in his tool belt for some big red pliers. He clamped them on the phone line to New York.

He worked steadily, and the crowd grew, but he ignored us. Like we were nothing to him.

Maybe that's why I finally yelled, "Hey, Bob, how's the view?"

A few people stopped craning their necks to look at me, somebody who knew him. They made a little space for me, like I was somehow involved.

Bob looked down.

He had one hand on the line to New York, and the other tugged the connection to Boston, ready to close the gap for a taxpayer complaining about his refund and a worried mother pestering her son and a scam artist cut off in the middle of a deal — losing money by the minute — and several spouses stuck in shopping aisles phoning home to ask what brand of toilet paper to buy. All were being held up.

Somebody must have turned on the current.

The crowd gasped. You could see it travel through him. All of it.

His trapped hands glowed like Hiroshima. His hair was a corona of solar flares snaking out like Medusa. But his eyes were the worst part, looking down on us from above.

The people next to me turned away, covered their faces with their hands. But I wasn't quick enough.

He saw right through me.

THE HUMMINGBIRD PRIZE
FOR FLASH FICTION

The Hummingbird Prize for Flash Fiction

One of the highlights of our literary year is reading entries for the Hummingbird Prize. In less than a thousand words, writers convey worlds and emotions that are tangible. We rely on the keen eye of flash fiction master Bob Thurber to pick a winner. He has a hard job indeed. And we allow room for the editors to have a favourite too, included also for publication in this issue.

Bob's said that the winner, 'Just Down the Hall' by Jeanette Topar, had 'qualities that glowed in the dark atmosphere and sense of dread the story presents. Nicely done.'

And the editors think William Kaufmann's story is a real peach.

902

Jeanette Topar *has had short stories published in* The Southwest Review, The Greensboro Review, Skidrow Penthouse, Central PA Maga-zine, *and* Liars' League NYC. *You can listen to recordings of her stories performed at www.liarsleaguenyc.com. Her one-act comedies have won national playwriting competitions in New York, San Francisco, and elsewhere, and have been produced off Broadway. She has an MFA in fiction from Rutgers-Newark.*

Just Down the Hall

Truth was, Mrs Cole had become a little afraid of 9 0 2.

Late in the evenings she'd hear 9 0 2's footsteps slide across the tiled hallway, hesitating outside her door. "Is this my place?" her neighbour would ask. Mrs Cole would mute the volume on her TV and hold her breath as she sat quietly in her tidy living room waiting for the woman to shuffle away. The last few times Mrs Cole had encountered her, 9 0 2 was wearing nothing but a gray slip that blended with the colour of her skin and matched her hair — she appeared little more substantial than a shadow or dust mote hovering in the hall.

She couldn't remember when she began calling her next door neighbour '9 0 2' instead of her real name. They had never been close — Mrs Cole was a youthful 7 4 and 9 0 2 a good decade older. And a smoker. Even so, there was a time they used to offer each other a cheery 'hello', or 'have a nice day'.

One night Mrs Cole decided to hurry a bag of trash to the chute before the start of the local weather forecast. She listened at her door before opening it to make certain 9 0 2 wasn't out there. She'd already kicked off her shoes for the night and hunted around for them. Where had she left them? No matter. Just this once she'd sneak out in her bare feet.

9 0 2 surprised her in the hall. "Help," she whispered.

Mrs Cole wanted to pretend she hadn't heard the older woman's raspy plea. But what kind of person would she be to ignore someone in need? Even one who wore filthy slips and reeked of cigarettes?

"Please, look in my apartment," 9 0 2 beckoned.

Mrs Cole didn't like the sound of that. "What do you mean? Is it a spider or something?" She was just as afraid of spiders as the next person.

"Come see," sputtered 9 0 2. She wasn't wearing her teeth.

"I can barely understand you," said Mrs Cole.

9 0 2 stood there twisting a knot in the front of her slip.

Mrs Cole took a step backward, toward her own apartment. "What is it?" she asked.

"In there." 9 0 2 pointed to her door.

"Maybe we should get the super." Mrs Cole took another step back. She could hear, from her own door, the weatherman announcing the lead story about a big storm on the way. To be done with her, Mrs Cole said, "Alright. Alright. I'll have a quick look for you."

Just inside was the kitchenette area, the same layout as Mrs Cole's. But unlike her immaculate home, 9 0 2's sink was filled with dirty dishes — it was no surprise. Brown banana slices floated in a bowl of curdled milk.

As her eyes adjusted to the dimness, Mrs Cole saw that all the furniture was coated with a layer of fine, white dust, like a powdered donut. Even the floors were covered. Her footsteps kicked up a little cloud and made tracks, as if in new-fallen snow. Obviously 9 0 2 hadn't mopped for a very long time, because there were also paw prints, giving the appearance that her old cocker spaniel, who had died last winter, still wandered from room to room.

Nothing looked disturbed or out of place, though. "Well?" asked Mrs Cole.

"There's a *man* in here." 9 0 2 reached out with a trembling hand and hooked her arm in Mrs Cole's.

"That's just silly," Mrs Cole said, whispering now too.

"Up there." 9 0 2 pointed to the top of a cupboard. "See?"

"I don't see anything."

"I was reaching for a glass and he grabbed my hand."

"Ha!" Mrs Cole forced a laugh.

"He's on the top shelf."

"I don't have time for this," said Mrs Cole. "I'm very busy." She searched 9 0 2's face for some sign the old lady was teasing, but tears ran along the deep wrinkles around her eyes.

"Please climb up and check. Back in that corner. That's where I saw him."

"Who?"

"The little man."

Mrs Cole studied the cupboard. She was certain there couldn't be anyone up there. Still, she wasn't too quick to slide her hand into the dark recesses of the cabinet. What if a water bug had crawled back in there? Or a mouse? Or even a rat? Reason told her there was nothing. Unless ... a very short man had folded himself in half and was just waiting to spring out. 9 0 2's fear was so strong it was catching.

Quietly Mrs Cole dragged a chair over, took a deep breath to steady herself, and climbed up. She stretched her arms into the cupboard, groping in the dark, hoping moment by moment that nothing groped back. All she found were rusted jelly jars and an empty box of Cream of Wheat.

"But I know he's there," pleaded 9 0 2. "He must have gone inside the wall. He does that sometimes. As soon as you're not looking, he'll come right back out," she cried.

"Well, he's gone now," said Mrs Cole.

"Look in the next cabinet."

"And I'll be going too."

"He's gone back in the wall. Behind the cabinet."

"It's OK. There's no one there."

"He'll be back."

"Good night," said Mrs Cole.

"How will I be able to sleep?"

Back in her own apartment, Mrs Cole fixed herself a cup of hot chamomile and settled in to watch the news. She quietly cursed 9 0 2 for making her miss the update on the storm. Now she had no idea what was heading her way. As she gazed about, appreciating the cleanliness of her living room, she noticed a trail of powdery white footprints across her floor. She leaned forward for a closer look. "Now, how did those get there?" she muttered. She didn't recall having any visitors. She sipped her tea and sat back, certain that tomorrow she'd remember.

William Kaufmann's *passion for writing is matched only by his passion for clay. He is an award-winning potter working in Western Wisconsin (lindenhillspottery.com). His recently completed first novel,* The Change, *won the 2017 SDSU Conference Choice Award and is being shopped by Trident Media for publication.*

THE BRUISED PEACH

Suit moved his briefcase between shiny wingtips as Tank pressed his body next to him on the pew-like bench in the train station. Suit slid over, putting a little distance between his pressed pants and Tank's slightly damp, mouldy clothing. Tank dropped a large wet black plastic bag on the floor in front of him with the sound of a thousand dented bells. Suits of every kind were on their way to work, briefcases in hand, ties tied in perfect Windsor knots. To Tank they all looked the same. They were all going somewhere. Tank had arrived.

"It's raining outside, if ya didn't know." Tank looked over at Suit. A cop across the way stared at Tank. "Hey, that pin on your lapel, that real gold?" Tank's yellowed teeth were outlined by thick cracked lips that broke into a smile, his eyes deep with wrinkles radiating from the corners. A voice like a rasp. "Wanna trade it?"

Suit's answer was silence. Eyes straight forward. He closed the gap between his shoes and his briefcase and stared at his cell.

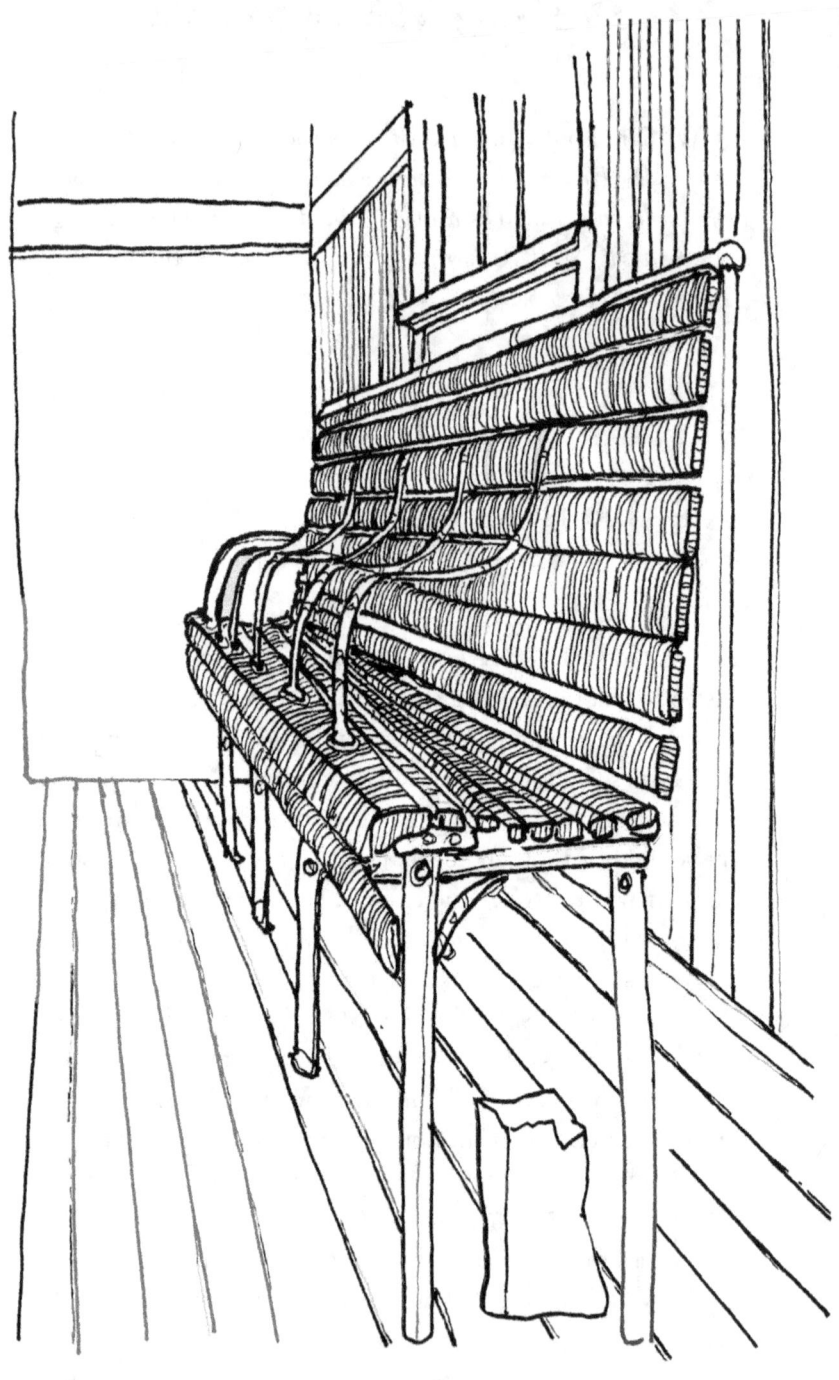

Tank ignored the silence. "My ma had somethin' just like that pin. Yes, sir, it's an American flag, ain't it?" Tank wiped his face with a rag from his pocket. "Some soldier boys showed up one day at our apartment and presented a real flag, like it was some reward or great honour to have your man killed by somethin' other than a neighbourhood bullet." Tank took out a pack of matches. "You wouldn't happen to have a smoke?" Suit shook his head. "Course not." Tank put the matches back in his wet pocket. "Walked all the way from 57th Street. What a downpour." He stuffed the rag in a side coat pocket.

Suit looked across the vast domed ceiling of the station as ten thousand bodies scurried for the next train. Giant circular windows high above spread an Eastern light over the cavernous expanse. Their wooden bench fell in the shadow of a giant pillar.

"It's like a damn cathedral, ain't it?" Tank followed Suit's eyes. "Them soldier boys left the flag, but there weren't any service for pa," Tank continued. "And ma? She bounced from job to job trying to keep us kids going. Mostly cleaned houses ... like the kind you live in. Ma worked late. She'd tiptoe in and say goodnight, make sure we were all covered, then drag herself to bed, and do it all over again the next day."

The cop looked over at their bench and adjusted his nightstick, looking at Suit. Tank folded his worn hands and leaned forward.

"I didn't turn out so good, suppose that goes just for the saying. I tried, but I couldn't do your gig. You probably think you know my kind." Tank chortled. "The same way I probably think I know your kind too. Bit of irony, eh?" Tank pulled a deeply bruised peach out of his pocket, the kind a grocer would throw out.

"I worked picking peaches for a summer," Tank went on. Suit

crossed his legs, moving his briefcase away from where Tank sat. "I can't tell you how many bruised ones get tossed. Some not even as bad as this." He held it up. "You know it doesn't take much to damage a peach. One drop and it can get a big ol' purple spot. Yet those dropped ones, I'd bring 'em home and eat 'em. Some were pretty banged up, but so damn juicy you could cut one over your cereal and not even use milk. And they'd get thrown. Like they were worth nothin', and just over a goddamn bruise. Can you imagine that?"

Tank shifted his eyes off Suit to check out the cop who was drifting their way. The cop wasn't in a hurry, just causally making a pass.

"Ma came home late one night with a purple welt on her face. Took a long time for me to figure out she did more than clean houses." Tank turned the soft mushy fruit in his hand, then looked down at the floor. "But I can tell you, mister, more than once she'd put that purple cheek next to mine with the sweetest kiss a young boy could own."

Tank held up the discoloured peach as if toasting with champagne or a fine wine, and took a bite. Juice flowed down his chin as he smacked it down with a smile. "Some of the best damn peaches are the bruised ones," he said, his words slightly garbled in his full mouth.

For a moment their eyes locked, as though some secret had been passed between them. "It's just life," Tank said as he wiped juice from his chin with his sleeve.

"Tank!" The officer waved. "Get over here." Tank got up, leaving the peach on the seat as if it would reserve his place. "Take that sack of shit and get out of here. And stop bothering people."

"Yes, sir, officer." He made a little bow and returned to his seat. Suit was gone, already halfway across the wide station. There was a shiny object sticking out of his half-eaten peach. Tank smiled, stuck it on his pocket, and grabbed the oversized plastic bag, cans clunking to the sound of misshapen chords.

Raising the peach in the direction of the rapidly disappearing Suit, he murmured, "To all the goddamn bruised peaches." And smacked down another mouthful as he left the station.

AFLOAT

Gabriel Craven and
Mikayla Fawcett

Gabriel Craven *is a comic artist from Steveston, BC. He has an unabashed love of the pulpy side of speculative fiction, especially that which deals with post-apocalyptic wastelands.*
Mikayla Fawcett *is a writer and artist currently emerging from a mudflat within the unceded territories of the Coast Salish peoples. Occasionally Mikayla emerges from the mudflat to engage in a larger collaborative art project.*
A*float is a short story set in a post-apocalyptic Canadian wasteland, part of a larger collection of related stories set in the same world under the title of The Here After Now. More post-apocalyptic comics from Gabriel and Mikayla can be found at TheHereAfterNow.ca.*

THE
HERE,
AFTER
NOW.

AFLOAT.

It's good to be out on the water.
We've gotten used to huddling close to the ground.
Spend too much time in the ruins, in the shadow of empty cities,
or in the settlements, under the tarp and scrap-yard roofs and laundry lines,
you forget what it's like to see the sky.
The last time I saw a sky this big was back home.
I grew up on the prairie.

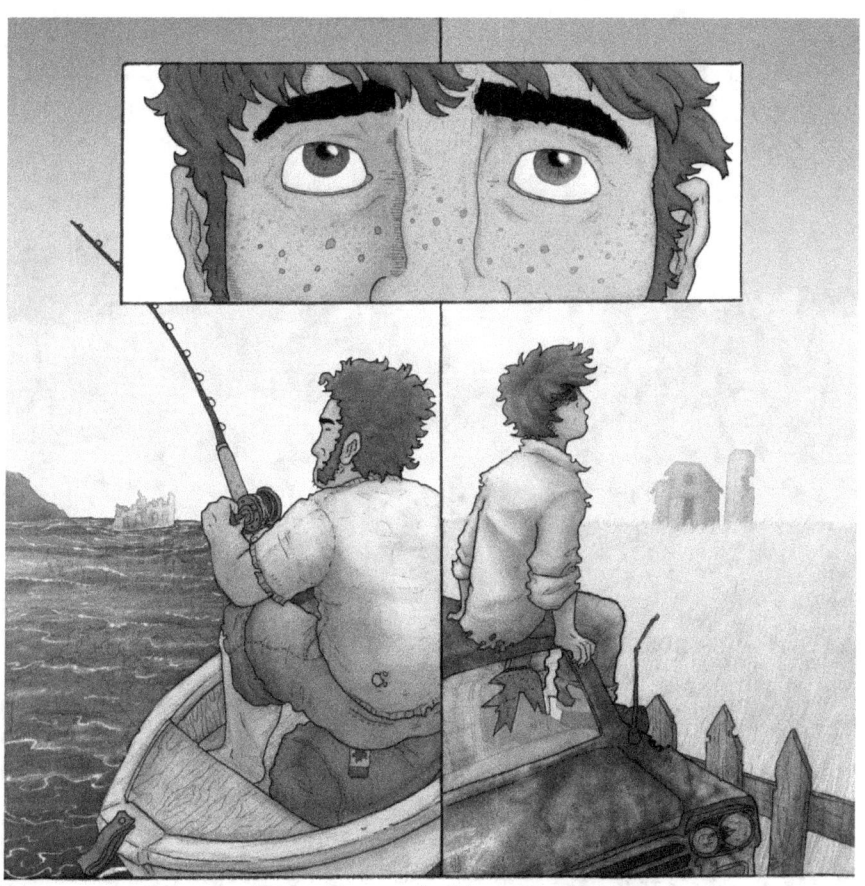

The world seemed so big even back then.
I'd heard about other places, other settlements, trading posts and ruins,
from my mum and other folks just passing through.
I wanted to see it all.
I learned everything I could about maps, stars, vehicles.
When my mum told me about the water, rivers leading to oceans,
and miles across the ocean a whole other stretch of land unseen in decades,
it was all I could do to picture all the field around me as water,
and me just floating.

They say the people from before could fly.
They had machines that flew through the air and carried them all over the world.
I wish I could believe it. I *did* believe it, until I saw the machines.
They're huge. Hulking monsters with guts like tunnels
full of chairs and windows. Tails like deformed fish,
and wide, outstretched arms folks call wings.

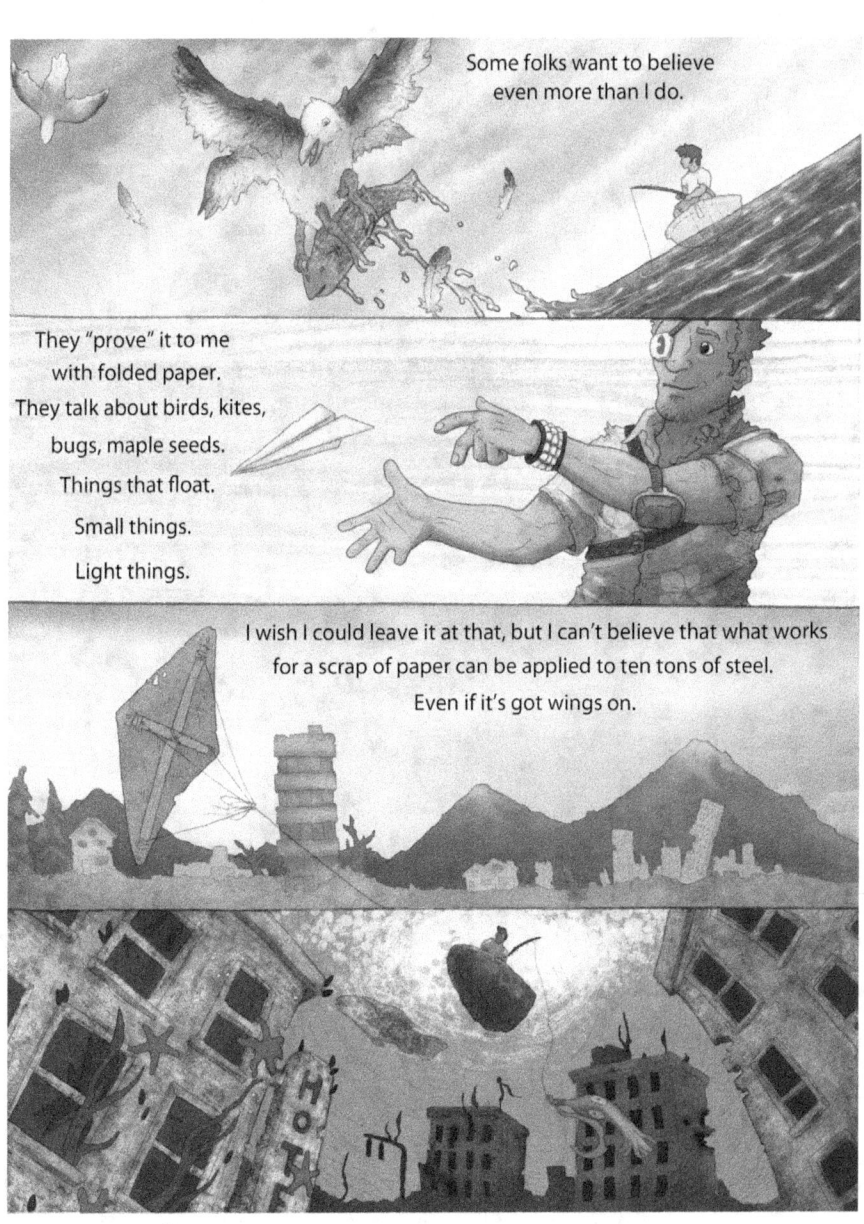

The believers always bring up the wings. They say,
"If they weren't made to fly, why were they built with wings?"
Maybe the builders, the people from before, liked the idea of flight as much as we do.
It's something to hang onto. If it gets folks looking up to see the sky, why complain?
Maybe one day they'll prove me wrong.
We'll take to the sky again. We'll know the actual size of the world.
I'd like that.
Until then, it's all I can do to picture all the water around me as air,
the drowned city below me dry and full of people going about their lives,
and me just floating.

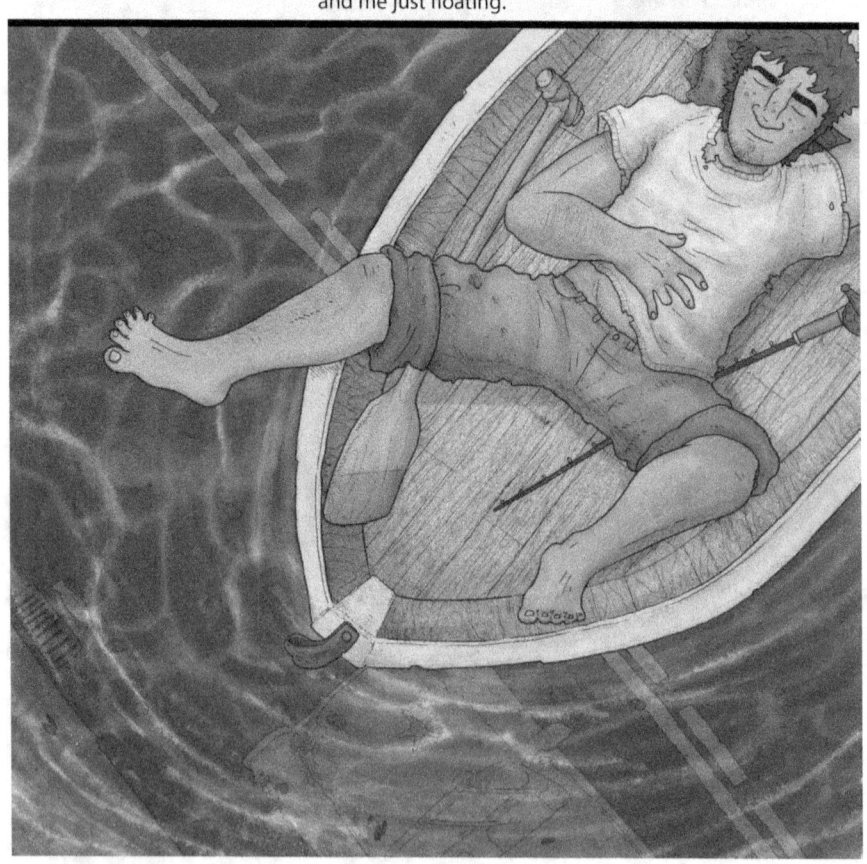

ALLAIGNA'S SONG: ARIA

JM Landels

Allaigna's Song: Aria *is the second novel in the* Allaigna's Song *trilogy by equestrian swordswoman, artist, and editor* **JM Landels**. *The first book,* Overture, *was printed serially in issues 1 through 11 of* Pulp Literature, *and is now available in a single volume from Pulp Literature Press.*

$\mathcal{P}$REVIOUSLY IN ALLAIGNA'S SONG ...

Fleeing an unwanted betrothal and enraged by her family's lies concerning her parenthood, fourteen-year-old Allaigna has set off to find her true father. However, her quest is interrupted a mere three days in when a chance encounter lands her in the illegal poaching encampment of her betrothed-to-be, Tiern Doniver. She is recognized but escapes, only to be brought in by Morran Rhoan, a travelling singer in the employ of Doniver.

Eleven years ago: Lauresa and her mother Irdaign have been reunited with the birth of Allaigna, and Irdaign has made herself a part of the household under the assumed name of Angeley. Lauresa struggles to forgive her and reconcile herself to her new role as mother, while Allaigna's happy childhood is upended by the birth of her brother Allenry.

$\mathcal{I}$RDAIGN'S CHORUS

Allaigna is still rocked back on her heels, her world pulled out from beneath her by the birth of her brother. No matter how a child likes the idea of a baby brother or sister, the reality is impossible for her to anticipate or adjust to easily. I comfort her small yet great hurts as best I can, assuring her she'll someday love her brother, hoping to plant the seeds that will grow to truth.

But I am preoccupied with preparations for the visit of my former husband. The urge to linger in Osthegn is nearly overwhelming. I could stay out of the way, remain ignored in the background, just to see him again. To see if he really has changed so much. My heart contracts, though I'd thought it had long since ceased to do so for him, especially after what he did to our daughter. But the mark of true love is that it can be smothered, forgotten, blinded, and waylaid, but it is impossible to extinguish. And for that reason, if no other, I must not stay at Osthegn. The risk of discovery is too great.

Lauresa is ambivalent regarding her father's impending visit. She is agitated, unable to sit. Her sudden rise from the chair by the fire wakes Allenry, but that merely provides her the excuse to pace back and forth, jiggling him.

"But why now? He's never felt the need to come before. Not for my wedding, not when . . ." She glances over at Allaigna, who is lining up wooden chess pieces on the hearth like a choir, or perhaps rows of soldiers.

I motion to Lauresa to follow me to the window seat on the far side of the great curtained bed. We can see Allaigna through the open curtains, but the quiet chatter of her monologue is muffled by drapery.

"He was ill for a long time after your wedding, Lauresa," I murmur, "both in body and mind. The guilt —"

"Guilt?" breaks in Lauresa, louder, I think, than she wanted. She glances at her daughter, but Allaigna still plays blithely by herself. "Over what?"

I weigh my reply before it escapes my lips.

"He married you off to a foreign lord, sent you on a journey that nearly killed you. For more than two weeks he thought it had. How might you think that sits on a man's conscience?

"If it was enough to make him ill, he might have reconsidered before actually sending me." Lauresa's voice is brittle. "What sort of illness, anyway?"

I turn my eyes toward the window so as not to have to look at my daughter. "An illness of the mind, my love. You must not judge him too harshly. It is likely he was suffering from it long before you left home."

"How long?" I can hear from her voice that Lauresa is taken aback.

Chanist showered her with affection when he was around. And when he was not . . . he simply was not. Had her memories not been clouded, she might have questioned his absences. But then again, she had been an adolescent, with all the self-centredness that implied.

"Still." She pulls back to the original subject. "Why now? Is this truly the first need he's had of a diplomatic visit to Aerach in five years?"

"Perhaps it is the first in which he'll have the time to stop and see you." I raise a hand to silence further argument. "In any case, it is imperative he not encounter me, so while he is here in Teillai, I will be in Aleran. There are many supplies I can't find here, and this is as good an excuse as any to make the trip."

Lauresa will not be silenced, though. "Why must he not know? What harm could possibly come now? And don't you want to see him again?"

I feel my eyes water despite myself. "I will see him again, but not now."

I refocus. "And do you think Gwannyn would allow him to visit you if she knew I were here?"

Lauresa's head jerks back as if slapped. As if the thought has never occurred to her before.

"Could she stop him? He is Prince of Brandishear!"

"Oh, I think she could quite easily," I reply. "But you tell me. You know her better than I do."

My daughter's frown increases as she realizes, for the first time in her life, who truly rules Brandishear.

What I have told Lauresa is true: there will be a time when Chanist and I meet again. It may even be within these walls. But the details of that future encounter are still unclear to me, hazed with a worrying sense of peril and change. I can do nothing but wait. I can see the present at will, regardless of distance, but the future only comes to me when it wants to.

Back in my workroom, I deride my wandering thoughts and continue to prepare the ingredients. The tincture I make for Lauresa to administer to her father I have made once before. It was when Lauresa was sixteen, not long after the birth of her cousin Genissa's baby, when the shutters of Chanist's mind first began to swing in the breeze of madness. I am still unsure what caused that loss of reason, for it was well covered up by Gwannyn and her advisors, and not a breath of it reached beyond the walls of the Royal Apartments — except for the words dear Ceilaf gave his young squire to carry to me.

I prepared this potion then, and Ceilaf ensured Chanist received it. It worked. It slaked the Prince's madness for a time, and, as Einavar later told me, perhaps saved a life or two. Now I have no insider within the Bastion. Ceilaf is dead, and that pain still burns when I think of his sacrifice. Lauresa's old nurse Dennein has been dismissed now that the last of Gwannyn's children have grown. So Chanist will have to come here, to my demesne. Where, if I cannot tend his sanity myself, I can at least leave the task in my daughter's hands.

VERSE 8

MORRAN RHOAN

"The lad is in my employ," Doniver informed Rhoan as he handed me back to my original escort. "But I prefer it if he appears to be in yours. I understand he can sing a bit — you might find him useful."

"The message, milord," I reminded him.

"The message?"

I scowled as much as I dared.

"Ah, yes," he recalled. "You're to carry word to a pair of vagabonds — the boy will tell you their location — and inform them I hereby lift all burden of obligation and debt. They are free from service, and I will press no charge upon them."

"And the papers, milord."

"Of course, of course." He reached into his doublet with a lazy gesture. "Give them these as well."

He passed Rhoan the two squares of parchment I had carefully read as he'd drafted and sealed them. Neither Raddick nor Dog could read, but if they kept these papers safe, they would hold Doniver to his word.

I was not a prisoner — not exactly. I had the run of White

Tooth and most of Castle Doniver. I imagine I could even have left if I wanted to. However, I knew the moment I did so, messages would go out to Teillai and rangers would be on my trail by the time I walked through the city gates. I was a prisoner of unspoken threats.

Morran Rhoan delivered the message and the papers, or so he said, and the words he carried back to me from Raddick gave me cause to believe him.

"The scruffy gentleman said nothing but clicked and gestured. I suspect him to be mute," said Rhoan, slinging his gloves and riding cloak carelessly over the bench and stretching his long legs out before the fire. Though the day had been warm, the spring nights were still cold. "The slightly less ragged lad babbled confusedly for a bit."

I was surprised at the warm rush of relief I felt at hearing Raddick had indeed made it safely back. I'd only known him and Dog three days, but our brief and intense sojourn in the woods had made me oddly protective of them, and of Raddick in particular.

Rhoan continued. "When he finally began making sense he commended himself to you." He paused with a performer's flair. "Let me see if I can remember the words. 'Oi'm indebted to … er … 'im, body and soul.'"

It was a great exaggeration of Raddick's rural accent, but Rhoan delivered it with such an accurate portrayal of the boy's hat-twisting hands and perpetually surprised eyebrows that I couldn't help but smile.

"And he sent me back with a jug-headed, sway-backed creature he claims is yours."

My heart jumped.

"I left him in the stables, but you'll have to pay his board, I'm afraid. Favours only go so far."

I hadn't dreamed of getting Nag back. I'd assumed Dog and Raddick would simply take him as theirs, and I was prepared to let them have him with my blessing. That Raddick had returned him with no thought to his own gain both warmed and saddened me.

"And ..." I hardly dared ask. "My tack?"

"In the stables as well, of course. Oh, and I suppose you want these." He reached behind the settle and pulled out the bundle he'd dropped there upon entering.

I turned to the bundle of my belongings: my bedroll, my bow wrapped in waxed cloth, my quiver. Rhoan reached over my shoulder and picked up the green-and-gold-scabbarded sword. He drew it halfway, peering at the ripples of watered Ilvan steel.

"Where does a poor apprentice singer get a pretty little pig-sticker like this?" he mused. His choice of the word 'pig-sticker' made me wonder what exactly he had learned from either Doniver or Raddick about my adventures of the past week. "None of my business, I'll be bound," he concluded, though I could tell already that his was a personality which would leave no mystery unearthed for long. He clacked the blade home in its scabbard and tossed it to me.

"This may be none of my business either," he said as I caught the sword, more grateful than ever to have it back in my hands. He leaned forward in a swift motion, like a bird targeting a worm: "But tell me, does the young Lord Doniver know you're a girl?"

I jerked back, fumbling in my head for an answer.

If I told him yes, what did that indicate about my relationship with Doniver? More than I wanted known.

"No," I lied, hoping to deflect further inquiry. "How did you know?" Maybe asking would flatter him. I was so deeply embroiled in lies, what was one more?

He laughed. "I'm not as blind as all that. Not as blind as you think Doniver is either. But rest assured, I did thoroughly rifle through your saddlebags to be sure."

He laughed again despite the mounting fury that must have been growing on my face. "Just so we both know where we stand. Or sit."

Although ostensibly Morran Rhoan's apprentice, I really had little to do during the day. My keeper slept till the noon bells most days, spent his afternoons I know not where, and appeared back in the great hall in time to sing and tell stories for the evening.

He surprised me one afternoon when he strolled into the archery yard as I was sinking goose-feathered shafts into a butt with a dull rhythm born of boredom and frustration.

"You're a fair shot for such a slight g—I mean lad," he whispered behind me, making my shot go wide and skitter across the ground, scattering hens who'd wandered out from the kitchen coops.

I glared at him and ran to retrieve the arrow. He twisted the others from the straw of the butt and handed them to me with elaborate courtesy.

"Where did you learn to shoot like that?"

I pretended not to hear him, busying myself with examining the fletch on the misfired arrow.

"And where did you get such a lovely bow?" He took it from

where it leant against my thigh and turned it over, testing the pull and eyeing the wood. "Elalantar work, if I'm not mistaken."

I snatched it back. Rhiadne had given me that bow. I hadn't seen her since she'd taken a captaincy in Brandishear. Thinking about the woman who'd taught me to hunt and track like a ranger, and who'd treated me like a younger sister rather than a duke's daughter, put a lump in my throat I could do without.

"Interesting," Rhoan continued. "I had one very similar, once. Harwen Elsing. They're very rare. His daughter gave it to me." His face looked different somehow. Sad, almost. "I lost it not long after I lost her."

On the base of the grip of my bow, right below where one's little finger sat, were the initials *H and E*. They were entwined with plants and a pair of chasing hounds, making them hard to see unless you knew where to look. I remembered Rhiadne showing them to me the day I shot three bull's-eyes in a row, and she gave me that bow.

"There," Rhiadne had said. "My father's mark. He's famous in Elalantar—and across the Ilmar. One of the finest bowyers and fletchers outside the Valnirata. Or at least he was."

"Was?" I asked. "Is he dead?" Back then, at the age of nine, I had very little in the way of tact.

She shook her head, a bitter look crossing her face. "You can't make a bow with only one hand."

I waited for her to explain, but she said nothing.

"It's pretty," I said, to break the uneasy silence.

"It's more than that," she agreed, her eyes seeming moist. "It's exquisite. It's the first one he ever made for me. It doesn't have the range of this"—she stroked the pale wood of her five foot tall longbow—"or even that." She pointed to the curved cavalry bow leaning against the stone wall. "I've not used it in years, yet still I carry it with me.

"But a bow should be used, Allaigna. The wood grows stiff and cracks if it is not. And a tool not used for its purpose is a vain and wasteful thing. I want you to have it."

I took the well-loved wood from her hands, hardly aware at that tender age of the great gift she'd given me.

Back in the present I eyed Rhoan. I wanted to ask how he knew Rhiadne, and if it was before or after I had. But those sorts of questions would reveal far too much about me. I unstrung the bow, gathered my arrows, and bid good afternoon to Morran Rhoan.

Later that afternoon I sat in the quarters I shared with Rhoan, running an oily rag back and forth across the carved shaft of my bow. The whorls and lumps of the pattern were as familiar and soothing as the turned posts of my bed back in Osthegn or the cracked and dimpled wood of my mazer.

That Doniver allowed me to retain my weapons seemed to say I was no prisoner. And yet I was not free to walk out of White Tooth. How long, I wondered, was he planning to keep me here? How good was his promise not to advertise my presence? And what would he extract from me in return?

It was all I could do to sit and calmly clean my weapons rather than bolting for the stables and riding out, no matter the pursuit. But doing so would only ensure I would become a prisoner in fact rather than in theory. I needed an ally, and the most likely, drunken dilettante though he was, was Morran Rhoan.

Before I could decide to trust him, I needed to know more about him, and to do that, I had to befriend him. It wasn't in my nature, but it was something I'd learned from watching

Garæthiel, and, I realized with an old stab of pain, from Goff. Those two could make friends of almost anyone. A shared confidence, a point in common, some small form of connection was all it took.

Until now, there had been no connection I could make with Rhoan. I knew nothing about him other than that he slept late, drank late, and was a musician of at least moderate skill. My ability to sing was far too personal, and too linked to the talent I didn't dare advertise, to serve as common ground. But the bow … that was my way in.

Using a silvered glass I'd 'borrowed' from the Dowager's lady's maid, I adjusted my appearance. It was a fine balance between maintaining my current boy's guise and allowing enough girl-ishness to come through. I brushed my hair thoroughly for the first time since leaving home and washed my face more carefully than I had in nearly as long. I had only the clothes I'd left home with, but I sang a small ditty, whitening the stains on the shirt cuffs and generally making myself presentable. This alone didn't make me more feminine, just less grubby and offensive.

I bit my lip as I regarded myself in the glass, wondering if I should find some rouge to pink my cheeks and lips. But I wasn't trying to seduce him. I wanted him to feel sorry for me. Protective, even. Still, I loosened the laces at my collar more than usual. I didn't have cleavage to expose, but my blue-veined, too-white skin was vulnerable and young looking. I considered singing a glamour over myself to enhance the effect, to make him want to help me. But the truth was, though I knew in theory how such enchantments worked, I lacked the skill, as well as the knowledge of men's minds, to be sure of myself. As a final touch, I swept the rushes out of our apartment and replaced them with fresh ones, adding generous handfuls of dried rosemary and lavender for remembrance and love.

Nothing remained to do but sit and wait until he made his inebriated way back upstairs.

$\mathscr{L}$AURESA'S CHORUS

"Yes, Angeley. I know." Lauresa rolls her eyes at her mother, taking the vial of brown liquid. "A dram in his cup at least once a day. Preferably twice."

Angeley sighs and wraps her arms around herself, nodding. "Yes, you've got it. But it's not just the tonic. It's what you say and do that will affect the cure."

Her mother untwines her arms, taking Lauresa's hands in her own. "Be the loving daughter you once were. Smile, and be gentle with him." Her mother deliberately relaxes her brow, trying to erase the frown on her daughter's by example. It won't work, determines Lauresa.

"I know you have so much anger left." Angeley takes one hand and places it on her daughter's chest just above the milk-heavy breasts.

As much as I had towards you, Mother, Lauresa thinks.

"As much as you must still have for me." Angeley echoes her daughter's unspoken words uncannily. "But withhold it for now. If you must ... if you must release it, don't confront him till he's been here at least a few days."

Lauresa nods. "I understand. Allow your magic time to work."

Angeley shakes her head. "Not my magic," she insists. "Yours."

And before Lauresa can ask her what she means by that, her mother has enveloped her in a swift embrace and stepped out of the workroom *en route* to Aleran, leaving Lauresa truly alone and in charge of her castle for the first time since her daughter was born. It is a frightening yet heady feeling.

Chanist, Prince High of Brandishear, arrives in Aerach under the guise of a knight ambassador, insignificant enough not to be known widely, but important enough to have a retinue. If anyone remarks on how unusually large and well-equipped the retinue, they assume Ambassador Ceilaf, as he calls himself, to have a fat purse from long years of campaigning followed by long years of royal service. Which would have been true, Lauresa thinks, her chest contracting, if the real Ceilaf had lived so long.

It shocks and angers her to have the memory of the man who'd died in her service sullied by a convenient charade. It makes practical sense, but it only adds to the confusing mix of emotions battling for supremacy in Lauresa's heart as the herald announces his arrival.

He leaps down like a man of fewer years and strides across the yard, leaving the stable boy to catch the reins of the stallion.

"Lauresa …" His arms spread wide, as if for an embrace, before he recalls himself. "I mean, your Grace." He bends, sweeps off his hat, and kisses her hand. There is a mischievous glint in his eyes, and none, that she can see, of the madness her mother spoke of.

Still, she is wary. Not just because of the alleged madness, but because she still does not know how she feels about this man who sold her off to Andreg in return for power. Time has not healed all the wounds. But she can play her part.

"Ceilaf." She reaches her arms out, returning the embrace he stopped himself from giving. "It is so very good to see you again, my old friend." The statement is made for the benefit of the onlookers, but for the most part, it is true.

"**Lauresa**," calls Chanist, just as she's about to leave her father and his squire to sort out their baggage in the guest chamber.

He crosses to the door, out of range of the squire's hearing, and leans against the lintel.

"When might I see my grandchildren?" He's not a very tall man, and his eyes are level with Lauresa's, his bearded face and slightly beery breath a mixture of familiarity and uncomfortable distance. The jug of ale that was brought up when he arrived has been drained already, and only a small portion of that was taken by the squire to slake the dust of the road.

She leans away from his breath, wishing she felt happier about seeing her father for the first time in five years. Still, the watery blue eyes before her don't disguise the longing.

"Soon, Papa," she promises. "Allenry is still napping, and Allaigna should be, though she's probably playing with the litter of pups in the kennel. Why don't you rest and change from your travelling clothes" — and let that beer settle, she thinks — "and I'll bring them to you when they're both awake and clean."

And hope you are the same is the unspoken addendum.

She gives him a dutiful daughterly kiss on the cheek and closes the door after herself.

Her first destination is straight to the buttery to ensure that only very well-watered wine is sent to the guest chamber. Her next is the nursery, where, as she can tell from the ache in her breasts before she's halfway back up the stairs, Allenry is waiting for his lunch.

When the junior nurse brings Allaigna, filthy from the kennels and disgruntled at having been interrupted at play, Lauresa is still wrestling with her dilemma. Allenry has fallen back asleep at the breast, so Lauresa has to lean over him to kiss her daughter. The child squirms out of the embrace, prickly and put out.

"Allaigna, love, I need you to wash and put on your best gown."

Allaigna twists her face into a deeper scowl. "Why? I don't like it. It's itchy."

"There's someone I want you to meet."

The scowl twists deeper still, and the child glares at her mother but eventually complies.

The decision is still not made when Lauresa heads for the guest chamber with a shiny yet surly child in her train and a dozing baby in her arms.

She holds her breath, hoping her father is respectably awake. She sent a page to warn him of his family's imminent visit half an hour ago. That must have been enough time.

The held breath partially escapes as his voice, clear and loud, responds to her knock. There he is, in the large armchair by the hearth, clothed in fine court garb, as regal and yet welcoming as she remembers him from childhood.

She releases the rest of her breath and takes a long, slow one back in. The windows are open, the air is clear, and her decision is made. There have been enough lies surrounding her family. She will not add more to the burden, nor deny her children at least one honest relationship. Bad enough Allaigna knows her grandmother only as a nurse; bad enough she'll never know her father.

She touches her daughter's shoulder and whispers, "Curtsy," out of the corner of her mouth. The girl is still learning that skill and accomplishes it unwillingly, but with enough childish charm to widen Chanist's smile and bring one to Lauresa's lips as well.

"Allaigna, love, this is your grandfather."

Allaigna cocks her head to one side and stares at Chanist. "My grandfather is dead," she declares. "And the other one is the Prince of Bandi ... Brand ..."

"Brandishear," supplies Chanist, chuckling. "And since I'm still more or less alive, old though I might be, I must be the 'other one'."

He rises from his chair, makes a deep obeisance, and takes her small soft hand in his large square one, kissing the fingers.

"I am delighted to meet my only granddaughter at last, your Grace."

Lauresa is impressed with his charm. Any attempt at hugs or kisses would have instantly estranged her thorny daughter.

He straightens with a hand on his back. "Ouf. Alas, I'm out of practice — or perhaps too old — for such courtly manners." He winks at Allaigna, charming her all over again. "Shall we come to an arrangement? We shall not bow and curtsy to one another, and you may call me 'Grandpapa' if I need not call you 'your Grace'."

Allaigna solemnly weighs this offer and nods with a dignity beyond her years. "All right ... Grandpapa." The last word rolls out slowly, as if she tasted it first.

"Wonderful! And will you introduce me to your brother, your Gr — I mean, Allaigna?"

Her tiny shoulders slump a little as she remembers she's not

only two days, which is not enough time, according to Irdaign, to make drink intolerable. How she wishes her mother were here now. But of course, the web of lies must remain. Andreg must not know Angeley is Irdaign, and Chanist must not know his former wife lives here and not at Aldac.

His initial reaction to the taste of wine is overcome soon by the masculine camaraderie engendered by great draughts of the stuff and the constant replenishment of his cup. After the first cup he forgot he dislikes the taste, and after the third could not taste it at all, fine Myrwater red though it is.

The chatelaine in her also balks at this guzzling of expensive cellared wine, imported at considerable cost from the south of Brandishear. But of course her husband has his insecurities, and it will not do for him to serve her father any less a vintage than he would find at the table on a Rheran feast day. Never mind that it is Lauresa who has chosen this wine, fit it into the butler's budget, arranged its shipment, and overseen its delivery. Never mind that at this rate half the cask will be gone by tomorrow and none left for the autumn feast. Lauresa is no more than sipping. Red wine gives her a headache, and more than a glass will pass her hangover to Allenry. The last thing she needs is a cranky, dry-mouthed baby waking her in the early hours of morning. Especially with Angeley gone.

Her reverie is smashed by a roar of laughter which awakens Allenry from his nap in Andreg's bed. They are having this private dinner in Andreg's chamber, and Lauresa has placed the baby on the bed rather than take him up to her own rooms. She stands, scoops him up, and begins the bouncing sway now ingrained in her bones.

Chanist opens his arms.

"Here, give him to me, Resa."

She hesitates, but deems her father still sober enough to hold a baby. At least if he's sitting.

"No, don't get up, Father." She leans over and places the wuffling Allenry in Chanist's arms. The baby will want feeding soon, but for now he keeps the cup out of her father's hands.

Chanist leans back in his chair, a smile of contentment on his face. Allenry, miraculously, doesn't fuss but relaxes against his grandfather's chest. Maybe he's been knocked unconscious by the fumes, Lauresa thinks uncharitably.

"Ah, I've missed this," murmurs Chanist. "I love a sleepy baby … and babies love me … I could always get you to sleep on my chest when your mother was exhausted by your demands." He smiled and patted his chest. "Babies know they can't get anything but a warm place to sleep from this."

Lauresa glances at Andreg, who has been puzzled into silence. As proud as he is of his male heir, he generally prefers to show him off in the arms of his wife, as a matched set. He's probably only held Allenry half a dozen times in the boy's life. He is having a hard time reconciling the Prince of Brandishear with the delighted grandfather who rocks the babe back to sleep, looking for all the world like a grizzled nursemaid.

A swell of unleashed tears brims up beneath her eyes, both for the father she no longer has and the father her children will never have. At least they have a grandfather for now, however long that lasts.

Chanist echoes her thoughts. "I'm so sorry I never got to hold wee Allaigna like this." His eyes are wet, as if the quantities of wine he's consumed are leaking out.

"I'm sorry too, Father," she murmurs, though even those few

words clog her throat.

Andreg looks more and more uncomfortable. Family intimacy is not his strength, and he has become the intruder here.

Chanist reaches out with his free hand and touches Lauresa on the cheek. "You look so much like your mother. Sometimes I wonder if I left any mark on you at all."

It is a dangerous statement in Andreg's presence, with mention of Allaigna still hanging in the air. She catches the hand, holds it to her cheek.

"Your ears," she says with a smile, "and your temper."

He looks at her in surprise, pulls his hand free, and lifts the curtain of blonde curls that hangs over her shoulder. "My ears? Really?"

He drops the hair and feels his own ear—small, compact, and flat to the head like a seal's. "By Fingal, girl, I do believe you're right!" He laughs. "But just in shape, I hope ... not my tone-deafness?"

"Not quite as bad as you, Father," she laughs in reply. "I can carry a tune with a lot of other voices and instruments. But not like—" She hesitates, knowing she should not remember her mother well.

He finishes for her. "No one in the world has a voice like your mother's," he says softly.

She lets that lie, grieving for the first time for the wife her father has lost.

Allenis has taken the opportunity created by his exclusion to refill his cup and his father-in-law's. Lauresa shoots an angry scowl at him across the table. He half-closes his eyes, smiles languidly, and ignores her. Of course, he has no reason not to: she hasn't told him of her father's condition, and not only because she doesn't want to hand Brandishear's secrets into Aerach's hands. She can't bear to see her father's dignity reduced in her husband's eyes.

Chanist raises his hand, refusing the refilled cup. "Not while I hold such precious cargo." He pats the wheezy Allenry on the back, swaying from side to side. A tuneless humming emanates from his chest.

As if he's forgotten he's already said it, he repeats his earlier statement. "Such a shame, such a shame I missed so many of Allaigna's early years."

"Then you will have to do double duty, Father, to make up lost time. This is your first visit here since I've been wed. I hope it won't be your last."

This time it is Andreg's turn to look daggers at his spouse.

VERSE 9

Faces Past

Even in his drunken state, Morran Rhoan paused on the threshold of the apartment, his eye sharpening momentarily as he took in the subtle changes I'd wrought in the room and on myself.

"Glad yer up, boy," he slurred, dropping his heavy wooden

harp into my lap. "Y'can oil and restring that now, 'stead of lettin' it sit till morning like you usually do."

Though I resented the work and his incrimination, I was glad enough for something to occupy my hands. And the muted burr of the harp strings as I turned the instrument over would be useful as well.

He dropped his long form into the large, leather-lined chair by the fire, limbs sprawling as if to occupy all of the small anteroom.

"Stroke of luck finding you, boy-girl." He laughed at the angry look I shot him. "My small room wasn't nearly so nice as these." He waved a loose-boned hand about his head, indicating the three rooms that made our apartment. "Lucky for me he seems to want a close eye kept on you."

I forced a wide-eyed expression, and though I knew full well the answer, asked, "What do you mean?"

He lifted a lazy eyebrow at me. "Why move me from a poorly furnished room next to the great hall to these rather pleasant chambers unless he needed to keep you high in this tower?"

I could barely breathe. Rhoan was leading the conversation exactly where I wanted with no help from me at all, and I was now terrified a wrong word would send it off course.

"Unless ..." He glanced sharply at me, eyes clear through the fog of wine. "You said he doesn't know you're a girl?"

My eyes went as wide as I could make them. "I never told him," I whispered. It was true enough. "Why would I?"

"Why? Why ask me?" His voice slurred once more. "I don't even know why you want to dress as a boy, so I'm the least-informed person here." He leaned over the arm of the chair and peered at me foggily. "Why *do* you pretend to be a lad? I'm sure you'd be a much prettier girl."

My hand jumped to my throat, pulling the neck of my shirt together. This was not where I wanted to the conversation to go.

"Do you think he knows?" I pleaded, begging him to take the bait back to the intended trail.

"Well ..." He wiped a hand down the length of his face as he did when thinking, closing his eyes and drawing his long features down farther still. "Why else put you far away from the prying eyes of the hall?"

Because I'm his fiancée, I couldn't help thinking, hoping the thought wasn't as plain on my face as it was in my head.

"What did he tell you?" I asked.

I withstood the foggy gaze again. "That you are a runaway apprentice from Erelin. That he heard you sing one night and took pity on you. Rather than delivering you back to your old master, he delivered you to me. Out of the goodness of his heart. Though I've always suspected young Doniver has very little of that beneath his ribs.

"But," he continued, sagging back into the chair, "if he knows you're a girl, why ... why ..." He fell quiet, staring at me with the unnerving clarity that swept in and out of him.

It set me wondering myself. Surely Doniver would expect Rhoan to see through my disguise sooner or later. So was his promise to maintain my secret empty? Was he deliberately trying to expose me second-hand?

I had to know more about Rhoan before I could decide. I dropped the oily rag in the rushes and set his harp upright in my lap. Picking a string at random, I plucked it, testing the sound. No ... not that one.

Morran's gaze was still pointed toward me, but not at me.

As if he were staring through me.

I plucked another string, felt its resonance: yes, that one was part of it. Before the sound died I added one more string, but it was major. I muted it with my wrist, cursing inwardly. Angeley had trained my voice, and I'd taught myself to sing small spells, but I'd never learned to play the harp well enough to know from sight which strings could make the spell I needed.

Two more strings, plucked together … ah, these were right. I could feel the harmonics blend and intersect, waves colliding and multiplying. This would be so much easier if I could use my voice, but I needed to speak.

"The bowyer's daughter," I said, my voice so soft it barely rose above the rhythmic tapping on the two strings I'd chosen. "Was her name … Rhiadne?"

He blinked, his gaze sharpening again. I kept my fingers moving, a metronomic alternation between minor third and root, the fifth coming in like a drone every twelve counts. It took enormous concentration to keep it constant while talking and listening, even more to keep it soft and subtle, no more than the twiddle of idle fingers.

All signs of drunkenness were gone as the man focussed his dark eyes on me.

"What makes you … ask that, lass?" he said.

In the end, I didn't need to sing a spell to gain his trust. The mention of my old tutor unblocked some latent torrent within him. Their relationship dated from before Rhiadne had left Elalantar and crossed the *Brôna Cœbann* to sell her sword to House Andreg.

The Kingfisher Queen, as Elalantar's Princess High was

known, had summoned Rhiadne's father to court. Rhoan, besotted as only young lovers can be, had followed, playing his lute and composing maudlin ballads, while Rhiadne, scarcely older than I was now, occupied her time helping her father teach the young ladies of the court to shoot. One of these ladies had overheard a proclamation of Rhoan's adoration and mistaken it for something directed at her. That she was already enamoured of Rhoan helped her to this conclusion. The comedy of mistaken intent led to Rhoan being chased from Caella with the hired swords of the girl's father on his heels, and Rhiadne close on theirs. Where poetry could not warm her heart, his plight could. They fled together, taking ship for Brandishear. Their misfortune wasn't over, however, for the carrack was attacked by pirates. Rhoan was struck unconscious, stripped of his belongings, and left for dead on the wallowing deck of the ship. What happened to his lover, he never found out, though he returned to Elalantar and went by foot to every town between Farwiel and Sudry in search of her.

I knew the end of her story, though Rhiadne had never mentioned Rhoan's name to me. With her rich clothes she had been taken hostage. She maintained the pretence of noble birth for some time, knowing it might save her from rape at least. But when the pirates learned at last she had no ransomable value, she threw her lot in with them, her skills with the bow unprecedented among the ranks of most mariners. But she was no sailor and longed for the firm feel of land beneath her boots. So she left them on the Isle of Orey, from where she joined the first militia she came across. Her rise to lieutenant of the Duke's rangers was almost inevitable from there.

What coincidence, what strange confluence of fates had thrown

Rhoan on my path? I wondered darkly if it was the meddling of that self-styled Queen of Fates, my grandmother, extending her long arm yet again. I put that thought out of my head for the time being. Dwelling on her could drive a person mad.

Rhoan, though, wept for joy upon hearing Rhiadne was still alive, and from then on he was mine.

Now I needed to get around Tiern Doniver. Each day since he'd stationed me in his keep, he called me to his study sometime after the noonday meal. Still convinced I was on a diplomatic or espionage mission sanctioned by my father, he questioned me daily about the situation in the Valnirata. I truly knew nothing—less than he, in fact—but with a skill learned from Goff I turned his questions around, letting him suppose I'd given him answers. I was continually astonished it worked, yet I had little idea what else to do. Our discussions went something like this:

"My scouts have reported unusual activity on the eastern borders."

I would raise an eyebrow, leaning forward with interest. "Did your scouts identify their clan markings?"

He might shake his head.

"Dress, then? What marks did they wear?" It was a senseless question. I knew next to nothing about the clan tattoos or manner of dress.

He would reply, "They didn't report on such details."

I in turn might roll my eyes at such ignorance, secretly frustrated, for I wanted the information for myself as well.

"Is it Oskaniia, do you think?"

"How can I speculate without more details?" But my glance let him think he was right. And why not?

And so this cat-and-mouse game went: me pretending to

know something and him pretending to have only Aerach's good above his own advancement at heart. But on the ninth day, the game changed.

"I tire of this, Allaigna," he said, provocatively using my real name.

Suspicion froze my face. I waited, wondering what new snare he had set for me, but he simply stared, thumb and knuckle pulling at his lower lip, his eyes burning into and past mine, forcing me to ask.

"Tire of what?" As soon as I'd spoken, I realized my mistake. Our relationship had changed. I was relaxed enough to question him, and that familiarity meant he no longer had to step with care around me.

"This charade. This game of telling me nothing every day. Either you're a better spy than I would credit possible for a fifteen-year-old, or you're nothing more than a runaway I should send packing back to her parents."

There was nothing I could say to these twinned accusations, for I had worked hard to keep his assessment of me balanced between these thoughts. To tip the scales either way seemed precarious, and I had no idea which side held the greater peril.

"And also," he continued, "I'm tired of sitting face to face with a grubby boy. He waved toward a bundle of cloth sitting on the bench by the fire. "That ought to fit. Put it on, and we'll continue this conversation over dinner."

I moved to the bundle and unrolled it. It was a dress, used but fine, in House Doniver's colours of gold and vair. It probably belonged to one of his sisters. Or mistresses.

I crumpled it to my chest and spun back to face him.

"You swore to protect my anonymity," I hissed.

"In exchange for your cooperation and information. Do you feel you've fulfilled your end of the bargain?"

"As best I can." It was true, in a way.

"Well, your best, in this case, seems inadequate. I require more. And as lord of the castle in all but name, that is within my power to attain."

"What are you threatening?" I asked through clenched jaws.

"I'm threatening nothing, Allaigna. Only requesting your presence in a more amiable situation, over a meal, and with your true face."

"This is my face." As I said the words, I realized they were true. I was more at home in my boy's guise than I would be in any dress, no matter how fine.

"But not the one your father sold me, I'm afraid. Don't look so affronted. You came with a dowry of certain powers and privileges, but your bride price is as high as any in Aerach, including that of Vishod's bastard daughters."

I didn't want to ask, but couldn't stop myself. "Why?" My voice sounded despicably meek.

"Why indeed? Looking at what I have before me" — he drew his hands through the air, presenting me to myself — "I'm hard pressed to answer that."

I felt the blood rising in my cheeks, half in embarrassment, half in fury.

"It might be your valuable heritage as daughter of Aerach's rising military star or as granddaughter of Brandishear's well-established one. Oh, I know that part is not widely advertised, but you don't buy a mare without looking at the pedigree first."

The heat in my cheeks was all fury now.

"Or it might just be that your parents value you. Not beyond price — but nearly."

How wrong you are, I thought. That chilling thought slowed my rage, let me remain silent for three long breaths. At last I spoke.

"So you would trot me out in borrowed finery, assess my gaits, check my teeth?" *I warn you, though,* I continued in my head, *they are sharp.* My fingers twitched, wanting the sword that lay safely stowed in my room.

"I would have a better look at the *girl* I've agreed to marry, yes." His reply was mild, but the threat still felt present.

And if you don't like what you see? I thought. *Or worse, if you do?*

What was to stop him consummating the marriage early? It would ensure I'd not be married off to anyone else. And might lower the bride price my father could still demand.

Terrified, but determined not to show it, I folded the gown over my arm.

"And what if anyone sees me in this?"

"Wear a cloak and hood. There is a back stair that runs from the tower base to my apartment. I'll leave the door unlocked."

"And Rhoan? Will he not wonder where I am?"

Doniver looked at me, suddenly taken by a thought.

"Does he know who you are?"

"No."

"That you're a girl?"

I shook my head. Lying seemed so much easier these days.

"How unusually thick of him. If he spent less time in his cups, perhaps he would have you figured by now. But don't worry. I'll send notice I've put you to work in the library. He'll never miss you."

I nodded and left, my curtsy hardly hinted at.

This must not happen, I thought. The next thought was, *Tonight.*

It must be tonight.

§

Allaigna's Song: Aria *will continue in* Pulp Literature *Issue 18,* *Spring 2018.* Allaigna's Song: Overture *is available in print and eBook* *from Pulp Literature Press (pulpliterature.com) and Amazon.*

THE ARTISTS

Britt-Lise Newstead

Cover artist, The Patron Saint of the Inevitable Death of the Universe
Britt-Lise Newstead is a storyboard artist, concept artist, and illustrator. She spent most of the last four years drawing Romans and Barbarians fighting each other in her day job for Longbow Games, then spent time in Vancouver to work as a storyboard revisionist on *Transformers: Rescue Bots* with DHX Media. When she's not studying biology at the University of Dalhousie, she indulges in her more whimsical side with the SmART School and Illustration Master Class. Her website is brittnewstead.com.

Gabriel Craven & Mikayla Fawcett

Illustrators, 'Afloat'
Gabriel Craven is a comic artist from Steveston, BC. He has an unabashed love of the pulpy side of speculative fiction, especially that which deals with post-apocalyptic wastelands. Gabriel has resolved to bring a gentler touch to worlds that so often thrive on violence and aggression.

Mikayla Fawcett is a writer and artist currently residing on a mudflat within the unceded territories of the Coast Salish peoples. Occasionally Mikayla emerges from the mudflat to engage in a larger collaborative art project. They take heart from the steady pace at which nature reclaims its space, and spend a lot of time watching the remnants of abandoned structures sink into saltwater muck.

'Afloat' is a short story set in a post-apocalyptic Canadian wasteland, part of a larger collection of related stories set in the same world under the title of *The Here After Now*. 'Afloat' evolved through a series of long conversations on climate change, sunken cities, and the unlikelihood of human flight. In the world of *The Here After Now*, airplanes, like much of the junk left behind by those who came before, are mythologized historic relics that entice the wastelander's imagination but defy rational explanation. The process behind this story was intensely collaborative and conversational, especially in its initial stages. Gabriel set the scenes and provided all page layouts and ink illustrations; Mikayla put words to their conjoined ideas, fit those words into text form, and painted Gabriel's inks. Gabriel, who was for all practical purposes raised in a kayak, set the story on the water. Mikayla, who has spent many hours along the Trans-Canada Highway, placed Elliot's childhood out in the prairie. More post-apocalyptic comics can be found atTheHereAfterNow.ca.

MEL ANASTASIOU
In-house illustrator
Mel Anastasiou loves drawing for *Pulp Literature* because she loves the stories she illustrates. She draws in black and white, working from imagination and inspired by details from Renaissance compositions. You can find more illustrations, as well as writing tips and news about her books and novellas at melanastasiou.wordpress.com.

JM LANDELS
Illustrator, Allaigna's Song: Aria

JM Landels studied at the Cartoon Centre in London, UK, under David Lloyd (*V for Vendetta*) and Dougie Braithwaite (*Punisher*). Although she is a perennial doodler, she put down her pencils and brushes after giving birth to three children, but rapidly dusted them off when she realized *Pulp Literature* was going to be an illustrated magazine. She blogs sporadically at jmlandels.stiffbunnies.com.

CONTESTS

Pulp Literature runs four annual contests for poetry, flash fiction, and short stories. For contest guidelines, prizes and entry fees, see our website, pulpliterature.com/contests.

The Bumblebee Flash Fiction Contest
Contest opens: 1 January 2018
Deadline: 15 February 2018
Winner notified: 15 March 2018
Winner published in: Issue 19, Summer 2018
Prize: $300

The Magpie Award for Poetry
Contest opens: 1 March 2018
Deadline: 15 April 2018
Winner notified: 15 May 2018
Winner published in: Issue 20, Autumn 2018
Prize: $500

The Hummingbird Flash Fiction Prize
Contest opens: 1 May 2018
Deadline: 15 June 2018
Winner notified: 15 July 2018
Winner published in: Issue 21, Winter 2019
Prize: $300

The Raven Short Story Contest
Contest opens: 1 September 2018
Deadline: 15 October 2018
Winner notified: 15 November 2018
Winner published in: Issue 22, Spring 2019
Prize: $300

MARKETPLACE

SHANTI ARTS
PUBLISHING

PAPERBOY
A DYSFUNCTIONAL NOVEL

by
BOB THURBER

$17.95
www.shantiarts.com
207-837-5760
ISBN: 978-1-941830-34-5
or your favorite bookseller
(online or otherwise)
ebook on Amazon, iBooks, Google

Thirty Days Towards
An Extraordinary Volume

THE WRITER'S
BOON COMPANION

Mel Anastasiou

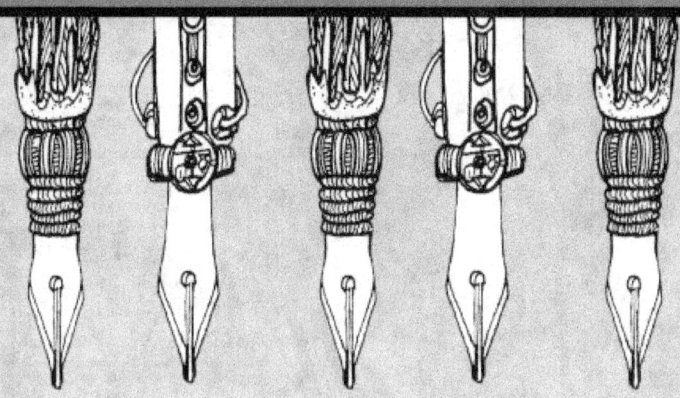

People's Co-op Bookstore

1391 Commercial Dr,
Vancouver, BC
V5L 3X5
(604) 253-6442
coopbks@telus.net

Regent Bookstore

5800 University Blvd,
Vancouver, BC
V6T 2E4
(604) 228-1820
regentbookstore.com

Village Books & Coffeeshop

130-12031 First Ave,
Richmond, BC
V7E 3M1
(604) 272-6601
villagebooks@shaw.ca

White Dwarf/Dead Write Books

3715 West 10th Ave,
Vancouver, BC
V6R 2G5
(604) 228-8223
whitedwarf@deadwrite.com

Conferences & Events

Surrey International Writers' Conference
October 2018
Surrey, BC
siwc.ca

Creative Ink Festival
for writers, artists & readers
18-20 May 2018,
Burnaby, BC
Creativeinkfestival.com

Magazines

Geist
Ideas + Culture • Made in Canada
geist.com

Mystery Weekly Magazine
The cutting edge of short mystery fiction
www.mysteryweekly.com

Neo-opsis
Canadian magazine of science fiction, based in Victoria, BC
neo-opsis.ca

Polar Borealis
Paying market for new Canadian SF&F writers & artists
polarborealis.ca

Room Magazine
Literature, Art, and Feminism since 1975
roommagazine.com

<small>P</small>RINTING & P<small>UBLISHING</small>
First Choice Books / Victoria Bindery
Book Printing & Binding
Graphic Design · eBooks
Marketing Materials
1-800-957-0561
firstchoicebooks.ca

Wesbrook Bay Publishing
Beverley Boissery, author and publisher
wesbrookbaybooks.com

Dear Geist...

I have been writing and rewriting a creative non-fiction story for about a year. How do I know when the story is ready to send out?

—Teetering, Gimli MB

Which is correct, 4:00, four o'clock or 1600 h?
—Floria, Windsor ON

Dear Geist,
In my fiction writing workshop, one person said I should write a lot more about the dad character. Another person said that the dad character is superfluous and I should delete him. Both of these writers are very astute. Help!

—Dave, Red Deer AB

Advice for the Lit-Lorn

PULP
Literature

Four awards for genre-busting fiction and poetry

The Bumblebee Flash Fiction Contest
Deadline: 15 February
Prize: $300

The Magpie Award for Poetry
Deadline: 15 April
First Prize: $500

The Hummingbird Flash Fiction Prize
Deadline: 15 June
Prize: $300

The Raven Short Story Contest
Deadline: 15 October
Prize: $300

For more information visit: pulpliterature.com/contests

Short stories, poetry, and comics you can't put down.

ℬECOME A PATRON OF PULP LITERATURE!

By supporting *Pulp Literature* on Patreon with $2 or more per month, you will be laying the foundation for a secure future for the magazine, as well as ensuring you will never miss an issue! Your subscription includes four big issues of short stories, novellas, poetry, comics and novel excerpts delivered to your door or electronic mailbox each year.

Find us at patreon.com/pulplit
If you prefer to subscribe through our website go to pulpliterature. com/subscribe.

Or you can send a cheque with the form below to:
Subscriptions
Pulp Literature Press
8540 Elsmore Road, Richmond, BC V7C 2AI, Canada

Don't miss an issue!

- ❑ **Send me 2 years (8 issues) at the special rate of $80** (save $40)*
- ❑ **Send me 1 year (4 issues) for $50** (save $10)*
- ❑ **Send me 2 years of digital issues for $30** (save $9.92)
- ❑ **Send me 1 year of digital issues for $17.50** (save $2.47)

Name: _____
Address: _____
City: _____ Prov. / State: _____
Postal code: _____ Country:_____
Email: _____

❑	**Payment enclosed**	Make cheques payable in Canadian funds to S. Pieters.
❑	Bill me	Include email address for digital editions and Paypal billing, or subscribe at www.pulpliterature.com.
❑	New	
❑	Renewal	*for postage outside Canada add $16 per year in North America or $32 per year overseas.